THE NIGHTMARE STARTS LIKE THIS.

An annual conference of technology entrepreneurs and MIT computer scientists on Nantucket. A group of heavily armed extremists bent on fomenting a civil war. The ferry *Nighthawk* on a fogbound crossing from Cape Cod to the island with 205 passengers onboard.

None of the *Nighthawk*'s crew expected anything but a routine workday when they reported for duty that morning, but when the shooting started in the middle of Nantucket Sound it was up to them to protect the lives of the passengers and save their vessel from destruction. These professional mariners were mostly ordinary people, although there is often something a little offbeat about those who break away from lives ashore to work on the water, like:

Chief Mate Grant Butler, a long-ago windsurfing champion with grown children, who dreams of selling his house and sailing around the world with his wife.

Deckhand Dana McSorley, a high-spirited sailor with a red ponytail and a tragic past, who carries a razor-sharp sheath knife in the small of her back.

Ship's Cook Justin Boudreaux, who hustles pennies from the crew playing cards in the galley while serving bodacious gumbo straight out of the French Quarter.

Chief Engineer Bo Diddley Jacobs, a calm and thoughtful man who has sailed the Seven Seas aboard freighters and tankers but refuses to retire, who will defend his engine room like a fierce young lion.

Deckhand Lou Crosby, a former commercial fisherman hardened by decades of hauling nets, who grouses about new hires who won't pull their own weight, but never speaks of his own teenage military service.

Operations Manager Damien Dalzell, born into the Highland Steamboat Company, who will inherit millions unless he breaks away from the family business to pursue a forbidden romance.

Deli Manager Katarina Dalca, the Romanian beauty who will put her life on the line to speak for the passengers who have become the hostages of an insane messiah.

This is the crew of unique individuals that is adrift on a dead ship, cut off from civilization by pea-soup fog and miles of cold water, strong currents, and shifting shoals. Yet they must find a way to rise together to confront a rising tide of vile hatred before it consumes the lives of all souls onboard.

Only an author like D. S. Cooper, who worked on the water for forty years, could tell this story straight up from the deck plates, with intense realism and stunning action that will keep the reader cheering for the heroes and wondering who among the passengers and crew will live and who will die.

But remember, it is only a sailors' nightmare—
and pray it never happens this way.

NANTUCKET RAMPAGE

TERROR ON THE ISLAND FERRY

D. S. COOPER

Copyedited by Jennifer Blackwell-Yale

Print and e-book formatting by Maureen Cutajar
www.gopublished.com

Cover design by Ebook Launch
www.ebooklaunch.com

For more information:
www.dscooperbooks.com

Print ISBN: 978-09984100-6-7
Ebook ISBN: 978-0-9984100-7-4

Dedicated to
America's Professional Mariners

"How still,
How strangely still
The water is today.
It is not good
For water
To be so still that way."

– LANGSTON HUGHES

AUTHOR'S NOTE

The Massachusetts Steamship Authority is the regulatory body for all ferry operations from the Massachusetts mainland, which has granted itself a monopoly to operate all car-carrying ferries to Nantucket and Martha's Vineyard. The Highland Steamboat Company and the motor vessel *Nighthawk* are entirely fictional constructs.

These events never occurred. The crew, passengers, and antagonists depicted on these pages are all products of the author's imagination.

PROLOGUE

The Wheelhouse

Shrouded in fog, isolated and windswept, the Gray Lady of Massachusetts has always been a serene outpost on the edge of a chaotic world. The Wampanoag called it *Nanticoke*—Distant Land—where thousands of that nation took refuge from disease and marauding neighbors. Later, some free-thinking English settlers divorced themselves from the puritanical doctrines of the Bay Colony and embraced Quaker simplicity here, building unadorned cedar shingle homes even while the clean-burning oil rendered from the whales that they hunted lit the lamps of America's parlors and made Nantucket, at its zenith, the wealthiest place on Earth.

Weathered shingle houses remain the rule, although many are now vacation homes for billionaires and celebrities, to whom the island's casual ambience offers the deference of indifference—the royalty of Wall Street, Silicon Valley, and Hollywood hardly get a second glance when navigating the cobblestone streets in flip-flops and Bermuda shorts. The island's airport may overflow with private jets on a summer weekend, but most of the supplies, year-round residents, and tourists are transported from the mainland by water, across thirty miles of strong currents and shifting shoals. This is Nantucket Sound, and the vessels in this trade are large, comfortable, and fast. Each boat is equipped and maintained to the highest standards, but most would agree that their exceptional safety record has been achieved by virtue of a cadre of dedicated professional mariners.

Captain Thomas Chapman was the master of one such vessel. On this day early in June he was standing by in the wheelhouse of the car and passenger ferry *Nighthawk* in Hyannis Harbor, preparing for his first crossing of the day. While the first mate stood on the stern and loaded cars, trucks, and passengers into the boat, he worked alone in the wheelhouse with the quiet confidence of a man who had performed the rituals that mark the beginning of a voyage thousands of times, rechecking the currents, weather, and vessel traffic he would expect to encounter. Precisely at one minute before the hour he sounded a short toot on the ship's whistle and pulled back on the levers that put the two massive locomotive engines deep within the hull into reverse gear, pressing the stern securely against the boarding ramp. At the same time he used the bow thruster to press the vessel's port side against the clusters of wood pilings that lined the ferry slip. When the chains were off, and the mate called "all set" on his portable radio, he stopped the bow thruster and blew a prolonged blast on the ship's whistle. He then put both engines ahead and aimed the two hundred and forty feet of sculpted steel that was the motor vessel *Nighthawk* between the buoys that marked the winding channel out of Hyannis Harbor.

This was a typically foggy morning on Cape Cod, so without a word from the captain a crewmember appeared on the bow and began pointing to everything he heard or saw through the gray mist. Likewise another deckhand—a high-spirited young woman with a red ponytail trailing from her baseball cap and a sheath knife in the small of her back—reported to the wheelhouse and stood by to take the helm once the *Nighthawk* was clear of the channel.

There are many kinds of captains. The worst of them blame the company for everything, while others are bullies who lead by fear and intimidation. But Tom Chapman was a captain's captain—a gentleman captain—who was not known to raise his voice in anger. His most ardent display of displeasure was to silently pace the length and width of the wheelhouse whenever the boat was not departing on time to keep the schedule. He was tall and lean and always wore a pressed white shirt and tie. He had spent five decades on the water, starting when he was a teenager, so it was his undeniable competence and calm demeanor that served as the gravity to knit a crew tightly together.

"We're earning our keep today," the mate said when he came up to the wheelhouse with the tickets he had collected. Grant Butler was second-in-command and wore a less formal white shirt without a necktie. "Seventy-one cars and nine trucks. The passenger count is two hundred and five."

"Very good," Tom said, nodding in approval without diverting his attention from the radar screen.

"Should I take the watch on the return trip?" Grant said. Like all the mates on the Nantucket run, he was fully licensed to navigate the boat so that the captain could have a rest period during their ten- to twelve-hour workdays.

"That would be fine."

"Great. In that case I am going to make another round down below. Did you know that Damien is aboard this trip? Roland is sending him over to sort out some sort of snafu at our terminal on the island."

"Yes," Tom said. "Apparently our early morning boat off the island is having a problem loading over there. Ask him to come up if he has a minute."

"I'll do that," Grant said, keeping his voice low enough that it could not be heard by the deckhand standing nearby. "If I can pry him away from you-know-who down in the delicatessen."

The captain stepped away from the wheel after Grant departed and allowed the deckhand to pull up a stool so that she could sit while steering. Dana McSorley was an athletic woman in her early thirties who loved to play softball and barhop with lifelong friends in Provincetown on her days off. On duty she wore blue shorts and a blue polo shirt bearing the company logo. All that dark blue clothing—as Tom noticed, with no small amount of admiration—made her red ponytail and green eyes really stand out. Most of all he appreciated that she handled the ship's wheel with a light touch, using small increments of the rudder to keep the big magnetic compass on the console pinned to the assigned heading. Such finesse was required because the *Nighthawk* had been designed with power steering and unusually large rudders to give the vessel superb agility for maneuvering in narrow channels and small harbors. New crewmembers quickly learned that when the *Nighthawk* was making good speed through the water, sloppy steering would be rewarded by a wild, rolling ride—much to the displeasure of passengers and crew alike.

"This is a real *pea-souper*," Dana said, referring to the dense mist that had closed in around the boat, isolating all aboard from the outside world. This was sea-fog, seldom experienced inland and thick enough to slice with a knife, the old-timers used to say. The ancients believed it rose out of the water with the seasons, like weeds upon the oceans, whereas modern mariners knew that warm, moist air over cold water was the culprit. And that a gentle sea breeze pushing ordinary fog against a lee shore, making the mist heavier and denser, was the final ingredient of the pea soup variety.

"Welcome to springtime on Cape Cod," the captain said. While Dana steered, he was carefully monitoring the radar next to his chair—this was the latest color version with detail better than high-definition television—while taking an occasional glance at the depth sounder and the electronic chart display, which showed the *Nighthawk's* position, as determined by the constellation of global positioning satellites, as a little green boat inching across Nantucket Sound. The chart was a jumbled hash of numbers and symbols indicating depths and buoys, and rocks and wrecks, and shoals and channels, and a hundred other things, which made sense only to those who had learned to read these runes.

"Dana, how is your shoulder?"

"Better," she said. "The cortisone shots really helped—it doesn't hurt much anymore—except when I'm trying to sleep. But I've lost some range and strength."

"Do you think you might go back to tall ships someday?" It was well known that Dana's first love was working aboard sailing ships in the tourist and sea education trade.

"I'd like to. But honestly, Tom, I don't know—"

"You should think about staying with this company, Dana. It is a good job and it's a real pleasure having you onboard. You have a license and a good head on your shoulders. You could be working as mate with us soon, even captain in a few years."

"Thanks, Tom," Dana said, equally embarrassed and pleased by the praise. "That means a lot coming from you. It's nice to have options."

They were halfway across Nantucket Sound when the first troubling broadcast came across the very high frequency marine radio, with an officious voice that said, "Attention all mariners, the Captain of the Port has closed Nantucket Harbor to all vessel movements. All mariners are advised keep clear until further notice."

"What the hell?" Dana said. "What kind of crap is that?"

"I don't know," Tom said. "That's a new one on me."

When he picked up the microphone and hailed the Coast Guard, Tom said, "I have two hundred and five passengers onboard who paid for tickets to Nantucket."

"Sorry, Captain," the radio voice said. "The port is closed for at least three hours. You may stand off and wait for the channel to reopen, but you can't come through the jetties until the Captain of the Port gives the all-clear."

"Coast Guard," Tom said, "can you give me a reason for the closure?"

"Not at this time, *Nighthawk*. The Captain of the Port will issue a marine information broadcast shortly. For now, all vessels are required to stand clear until further notice."

"This is crazy," Tom said after he put down the microphone. "Damien was going to the island to sort out some problem at the terminal, so maybe he knows what is going on over there." He picked up the handset for the sound-powered telephone—the small gray boxes of the system were called "growlers" and were located at various places throughout the vessel—and he set the dial and turned the crank to ring the phone in the small kitchen between the delicatessen and the cocktail lounge, one deck below the wheelhouse. "Is the mate down there?" Tom said. "Put him on please." After a brief conversation with Grant, Tom set the handset back in its cradle and looked thoughtfully into the fog for a few moments before he looked at Dana. "Grant and Damien don't have any ideas," he said.

"What are you going to do?" Dana said.

"I can't hold the passengers hostage for hours," Tom said. "And I am not going to announce our dilemma to the main office over the radio, where the whole world will hear it. If we turn around toward Hyannis, we will be back within cell phone range of the office in a few minutes, so I can talk to Roland privately."

"He's going to say the same thing he always says—it's up to you, Captain."

"That's true," Tom said. "But it never hurts to inform the owner of problems before he hears it from someone else." He looked at the radar screen again. The ferry turning around in mid-crossing would be big news on the islands. It wouldn't be good for Roland to learn of the cancellation on WMVY radio, which broadcast adult progressive rock music and local news for the cape and islands, including crossing conditions for the ferries and the number of cars and trucks in standby. "Bring her about, Dana. Do so handsomely, please. We don't want to alarm the passengers. Not yet, anyway."

"Coming about, aye," Dana said. She turned the wheel just one spoke into a turn that she hoped the passengers would not notice in the fog.

When Tom cranked the growler phone again, he had the dial set to the crew's galley, and he said, "Better get ready to serve lunch early, Justin. We're going back to Hyannis—I'll explain later."

Only a few minutes passed before the bell on the growler vibrated with an incoming call. When Tom picked up the handset, he heard Grant say, "We have big trouble down here."

"Where is Judd?"

"That idiot is the trouble," Grant said. "Some nutcase grabbed Judd's gun and ran off with it. At least he was running away from the passengers, down to the freight deck. But this could get really ugly."

"Keep a lid on it," Tom said. Then he put down the handset and said, "I have the helm, Dana. Go aft and notify the off watch that we have trouble on the passenger deck. Tell them someone disarmed Judd and ran off with his gun, so be careful. Then I want you and Justin to lock all the doors to the galley and the crew's quarters from the inside so the troublemaker cannot get into the wheelhouse. Come right back here when that is done."

Dana bolted through the door into the passageway behind the wheelhouse, which was lined with small staterooms for the crew, spreading the alarm. The galley and mess-deck were behind a heavy steel fire door at the end of the passage. The off-duty crew were there playing cribbage with the cook.

"There's trouble down below," Dana said. "Somebody has Judd's gun. Tommy wants us to lock all the doors up here so no one can get into the wheelhouse."

"Let's go," one of the deckhands said. They threw down their cards and flew out the galley door, leaving cook Justin Boudreaux to turn down the heat on the large pot of gumbo that was cooking on his stove. He was a large man who, like some professional chefs, never allowed himself to be rushed and hurried in his kitchen.

"Sweet Jesus," Justin said, tossing his white apron aside with a slow sweep of his arm and words that flowed with a drawl out of the Deep South. "Can't I ever serve lunch on time? It's one gosh-darn thing after another on this boat."

Dana was back in the wheelhouse by the time Tom called the Coast Guard on the radio and said, "The motor vessel *Nighthawk* has trouble onboard and is en route back to Hyannis. My position is forty-one degrees and twenty-seven minutes north, seventy degrees and ten minutes west. Request you send help to us now and have law enforcement meet us at the ferry terminal."

"Negative, *Nighthawk*," the voice on the radio said. "Anchor your vessel and have all persons onboard put on life jackets."

"That's not the kind of help I need," Tom said. "You'd better come back with something better than that. I am en route to Hyannis so send help immediately."

Dana gasped when three gunshots were heard, followed by two more in rapid succession. These were loud, deep-throated reports of a big-bore weapon, which conveyed instant terror as they echoed around the boat in the fog.

"Damn it," Tom said as he hit the button to close the automatic fire doors between the forward and aft passenger compartments. Then he picked up the general announcing microphone, which would carry his words all through the vessel, and in his best radio voice he said, "Ladies and gentlemen, please remain calm and follow the instructions of the crew. Thank you."

"Oh my God," Dana said. "Should I go down and see what is happening?"

"Stay here, Dana," Tom said. "I need your help to get the boat back to Hyannis. That's where we can get the best help if we have some injured people."

"Is this for real, Cap?" Justin said, when he came to the wheelhouse with two large kitchen knives and a dough rolling pin.

"I'm afraid so," the captain said. "Lock all the exterior doors to the crews' quarters and stand by in the galley. I fear we are dealing with more than just some nutcase who grabbed Judd's pistol. Maybe we can keep them out of the wheelhouse long enough to get back to Hyannis."

"We're locked up tight, Cap. Take these."

"Just leave the rolling pin on the chart table," Tom said as he stepped in to take the helm. "Dana, go to the galley with Justin and lock yourselves in tight."

"I want to stay with you, Tom."

"Please do as I say. If they get into the wheelhouse through the galley, they can take control of the boat—then we would be helpless. I'm counting on you to stop them from getting in."

Justin said, "Nobody's going to get in through the galley, Cap. I promise you that."

"Just do your best for the boat," Tom said. "And take care of yourself if you can."

"Sweet Jesus," Justin said as he opened the door to leave the pilothouse. "Damn, Tommy, this is a real shitstorm, isn't it?"

"It's the worst," Tom said. "We have to remember our training and make the best of it."

"They're coming," Dana said as she looked out the aft-facing window on the side wing of the wheelhouse. "Two guys with guns are on the sundeck right now."

"Get to the galley," Tom said. "Barricade yourself in there with Justin."

"Good luck, Tom."

"Right. Good luck to us all."

Tom pushed the throttles down for full power from the engines. He had both hands on the wheel as he steered through the fog toward Hyannis Harbor, the outer precincts of which appeared on his radar screen as a green appendage under the arm of Cape Cod. Against all his instincts as a mariner, he was prepared to drive the *Nighthawk* into the sand on the beach and give everyone a chance to jump for it, if it came to that.

Tom knew he was out of time when he heard heavy footfalls on the roof of the pilothouse. Moments later a man holding a black assault rifle dropped down to the small deck in front of the windshield. The bore of the deadly weapon looked as large as a subway tunnel when it was pointed directly at him, but he did not cower—rather, Tom Chapman stood resolutely at his ship's helm, as he always had.

Jesus, Tom thought, without flinching. *I know that face—*

In an instant there was a brilliant flash from the muzzle of the ugly weapon and the explosive shattering of safety glass. Thus, did Captain Thomas Chapman's final trick at the helm end in eternal darkness.

EARLIER THAT MORNING

The ferry NIGHTHAWK
preparing to depart from Hyannis Harbor.

1

ROUTINE CROSSING

The Boarding Ramp

That old uneasy feeling came over Grant Butler that morning as it sometimes did when the vessel was operating a little too smoothly. Maybe it was that the crew was laughing and well rested when they reported for duty, or that the passengers were following instructions without complaint, or that all the machinery was in perfect condition. Sure, there would be some fog on the crossing, but it was nothing that the captain and crew could not handle.

It was not that Grant was pessimistic by nature—far from it. Like nearly all professional mariners, he had learned that when the job seemed too easy it was time to get your guard up. On the easy days he often found himself casting sideways glances for trouble. An engine might stick in gear and cause them to ram the dock, or the steering pumps could fail and send the *Nighthawk* veering into another vessel, or a passenger could slip and fall on the unforgiving steel stairways leading down from the passenger deck. But there were no signs of any such disaster brewing this day.

This was a Thursday, so he was working as mate on the motor vessel *Nighthawk*. On any Friday—which Tom Chapman usually took as a day off—he would be in the wheelhouse all day as relief captain. But Grant enjoyed his mate days more; the pay was nearly the same, and he was free to roam the boat doing maintenance, safety inspections, and solving whatever problems the crew or passengers might have.

Half an hour before departure the yard crew was lining up cars and trucks for the crossing. Grant came down to the stern and leaned against the railing alongside the boarding ramp. He had a few minutes before it was time to take tickets and load the boat, so he lit up his second—or was it the third?—cigarette of the day. The boats were a good job, but he had not come to them directly from a maritime academy or out of the Navy, as was so often the case. He had grown up in Falmouth and had worked as a lifeguard at the country club all through high school. He was only fifteen years old when he won his first windsurfing championship, so after graduation he worked as a windsurfing instructor, as well as a carpenter and at other odd jobs, and in the winter months he went to Colorado and worked as a ski instructor. When he took a job with the ferry company as a deckhand —he was then twenty-four years old—he had no expectation that it would last any longer than had his tenure as a carpenter or a landscaper. But the freedom and the challenge of working long hours on the water in all sorts of weather suited him, and the old hands had pressured him— "You're a smart kid, Grant. Hit the books and work your way up to the wheelhouse"—and soon he was sitting for his 100 ton license to operate the company's smallest boats, then his mate's certificate for larger vessels, and finally his captain's license was posted next to Tom's aboard the *Nighthawk* and it seemed that all the big decisions of his life had been made. Now all that remained was to get his two children through college and ease himself into semiretirement.

Maybe I can buy a bigger sailboat, he thought. Maybe Diane would really be willing to sell the house and sail around the world. Maybe.

"When are you going to quit those cancer sticks?" the engineer said when he limped up from the engine room and stood near Grant.

"I did quit them," Grant said, "at least twenty times."

"Go for twenty-one," the engineer said. Bo Diddley Jacobs was an older black man, long past retirement age but incapable of staying home when there was work to be done, in tattered coveralls that hung loosely on his lanky frame. His right leg had been mangled in some accident aboard an oil tanker years earlier, but he never let it slow him down. He spent his off time in his stateroom, reading all sorts of books. He spoke quietly and enunciated each word with care. "Maybe twenty-one is your lucky number."

It might have bothered Grant if someone else had nagged him about his smoking, but there was nothing supercilious about Bo, and his smile was genuine.

Twenty minutes before sailing time he snuffed out his cigarette and started boarding the walk-on passengers. Grant said hello and took a ticket from each person who passed his post. The tourists were okay, but he genuinely enjoyed the repeat customers, many of whom he had seen in passing once or twice a week for years. A familiar young girl in a plaid skirt with a Yorkie terrier in her arms said, "Good morning, Captain Grant." When she handed him her ticket, he patted the dog's head, and he asked if she had another ticket for the dog, which was a standing joke between them. It was also easy to talk to the sports fans in their Red Sox and Yankees hats, and to listen to complaints about traffic delays on the Bourne and Sagamore bridges, or to hear about the little trips to the mainland that island residents took for work, or to shop, or to visit a doctor's office. He might take a stock tip from a businessman, even though they both knew he would never follow up on it. He had watched children who first came aboard in their mother's arms grow up to be teenagers. That kid with the backpack and the Roger Williams University sweatshirt—wasn't it just yesterday that he was running ahead of his parents and being scolded to slow down? And sometimes Grant asked after a customer whom he had not seen for a time, only to be informed that they had entered a nursing home or passed away.

The security man came to the boarding ramp while Grant was taking tickets from the walk-ons. Horace Judd was a recent and somewhat unwelcome addition to the lineup of people who worked on the *Nighthawk*, a miserable man with pale sticks for legs, a bulbous stomach, and a paranoid streak up his back. He stood apart from Grant and Bo in his shooter's vest and amber sunglasses, putting a great deal of effort into attempting to look formidable.

"Good lord," Bo said. "He gets more ridiculous every day."

"Take it easy, Bo." Grant said, somewhat taken aback to hear the older man speak ill of anyone. "It's not like you to speak like that, and I think he might have heard you."

"I don't much care what he hears," Bo said. The old engineer dropped to one knee near the boarding ramp to disconnect two heavy hoses from pipes on the pier. The blue hose brought potable water aboard and the black tube carried gray water—sewage—off the boat. "I don't have much use for a man who doesn't pull his own weight on a boat."

"Let me get one of the deckhands to help you with those hoses," Grant said.

"Don't you go minding my load," Bo said. "The deckhands have their own work to do. What you ought to be minding is that I'm a tired-out old man who's working all day while a slacker with a gun is standing around waiting to hassle the customers."

"Judd works for an outside security company, Bo. He's not part of the crew, but we have to carry him because of the new regulations that require armed guards aboard passenger boats."

"Right," Bo said. "And now we're stuck with a lazy dolt with a gun. He eats in our crew galley and shits on our crew commode and does not lift a finger to clean up after himself. He's too busy suspecting anybody with dark skin or an accent that his narrow little mind doesn't particularly care for, like it's a crime for them to buy a ticket and come sit on the boat."

"I know," Grant said. "I'm not happy about the way Judd goes about his business, but he's just too dumb to know the difference between the way a person looks and the way they act."

By then it was time for Grant begin to loading cars and trucks into the *Nighthawk*'s cavernous freight deck, which had large doors at the bow to keep the seas out as the vessel cut through the waves, while the stern was wide open, to allow fresh air in and car exhausts to escape. The ferry was classed as a RORO—a roll-on/roll-off cargo and passenger vessel, meaning that cars and trucks could drive on at one end and off at the other. The freight deck was six lanes wide, with raised decks between the freight deck and the passenger deck—called 'tween decks—on each side. Each 'tween deck had two lanes for parking small- to medium-size cars, with steep ramps to drive up and down at both ends. Sedans and sport utility vehicles fit nicely into the two lanes under each 'tween deck, but the deckhands had to take great care in guiding customers around the steel support pillars underneath, which were all painted bright traffic yellow. If a customer got a little too close, they might lose one of their car's side-view mirrors, and if they got way too close, they would leave the boat with yellow stripes on their fenders. Islanders sometimes called these "day-tripper stripes."

There were six staircases on the freight deck leading up to the passenger deck, plus an elevator for those with mobility issues. The two main compartments above the freight deck had comfortable seats for three hundred customers, and above that was the wide-open sundeck, with wooden benches like church pews for sun worshippers and commanding views of Nantucket Sound on every fair-weather crossing.

As vehicles pulled up to the ramp, Grant took their tickets and directed each driver to a spot that was suited to the dimensions of their vehicles. When the 'tween decks and the car lanes underneath were full, he directed trucks to the two center lanes. Most were delivery trucks that went across nearly every day, or service vehicles that would stay on the island only long enough to complete some job. There was a low-boy flatbed tractor trailer with a bulldozer, and he recognized one old crew-cab pickup truck with dual rear wheels and Michigan license plates. The pickup had a dented aluminum cap over the bed, mud on the tires, and five rough-looking men in the cab, who had made the crossing several times in recent weeks. They were probably construction workers, very few of whom could afford to live on the island where their skills were in demand.

"Hey, buddy," the bearded driver of the work truck said, as he handed Grant his tickets. "Is this fog going to slow us down? We have a job to get to on the island."

"We'll do our best to keep to the schedule," Grant said. "We run in the fog almost every day." He noticed that the men looked a little anxious, as if they were concerned about making the crossing in restricted visibility. "You fellers are a long way from home for a job."

"There's not much work on the Upper Peninsula these days," the driver said.

"I hear that," Grant said as he waved the truck on. "We're all doing our best and making it any way we can. Go to the left side of the center section, please."

Grant had put most of the cars and trucks with reservations on the boat when he saw one of the owners of the Highland Steamboat Company leave the ticket office and come across the parking lot. Damien Dalzell was the youngest child of the family that owned a conglomeration of ferries, towboats, and a shipyard with a large dry dock, all of which amounted to the grandest multigenerational maritime enterprise in Southern New England. One year out of college, tall and slim, with dark brown eyes and black hair that was always neatly trimmed, he was already a millionaire by birth—although you wouldn't know it by the work boots and chinos he always wore on the job. There were rumors that he owned a Porsche convertible and cavorted like a playboy when he had a rare night off, but for the most part he and his siblings worked ten-hour days, six days a week, in the office and in the shipyard. When he reached the ramp, he waved hello to Grant and put down the notebook and bundle of papers he was carrying. Without a moment of hesitation or being asked to assist, Damien put on a pair of work gloves and kneeled on the boarding ramp to help Bo disconnect the water and sewage lines.

Damien was still down on one knee when Katarina Dalca walked onto the boat with some supplies for the delicatessen. She wore the same light blue shirt as all the deli workers, but she added some flair with a strip of pink silk at her neck and capri pants that hugged her long legs and guided men's eyes to the two perfect hemispheres of her buttocks, which twisted and rolled slightly with each of her narrow little strides.

Damien pretended not to hear Bo when he said, "You got to love a European lady," but Katarina turned her head slightly toward the men and smiled sweetly after she passed.

"Man, the way she walks," Bo said. "Graceful as a princess. Those Continental girls really class this place up."

"I guess they do," Damien said.

The last truck in line with a reservation for boarding was from a Boston catering company. The driver was a good-looking kid, maybe not more than twenty years old. "Hey, man," he said with a toothy smile. "This is screwed up. The ticket office told us we'd be at the front of the boat."

"If you want to be up front, you have to get here early and be first in line," Grant said. There was a man with tattoos and a baseball cap pulled low over his eyes sleeping in the passenger seat. "I need a walk-on ticket for your friend, too."

The driver found the ticket for his sleeping companion and handed it out the window to Grant. "Can't you back those other trucks off and put us in front?" the driver said. "The ticket office said we would be the first ones off on Nantucket."

"The ticket office doesn't load the boat, and there is no way I'm going to rearrange this load. We've got a schedule to keep."

"We have to be the first one off this boat," the driver said, as his passenger sank deeper into the seat and pulled his cap down to his chin. "We need to get to the yacht club before the buffet."

"I can't put you up there," Grant said. "Not only weren't you here first, the exhaust from that refrigeration unit over your cab will get soot on the overhead after the bow doors close, unless I keep you back here in the open end."

The young truck driver drove onto the boat and begrudgingly took his spot near the stern. With all the reservations onboard, there was only one spot left, and Grant took the first car in the standby line, a silver minivan with New York plates.

The family cruiser parked behind the catering truck and when the driver got out, he said, "Thanks for getting us on." He was clean-cut and fit and he looked directly at Grant when he spoke, clearly projecting his voice without raising the volume. Everything about his demeanor suggested that he was a military man, or a cop, or a firefighter.

"No worries," Grant said. "Enjoy the trip." He watched as the man herded two smiling boys—twins in New York Mets sweatshirts—to the stairs. His woman was a slim, attractive lady in jeans with no makeup, who went ahead carrying a toddler with curly blonde locks.

By then Tom had put the engines in reverse to hold the *Nighthawk* against the ramp and tooted the horn to signal, "time to go." When Grant turned around, he saw that Judd had confronted a late walk-on passenger, a young woman wearing a modest dress with a white hijab covering her head and a baby in her arms.

"I'll take your ticket, ma'am," Grant said, interrupting Judd's interrogation of the prospective passenger. The security man showed his displeasure with a disgusted scowl when Grant waved the woman aboard and said, "Enjoy the trip."

With the last passenger aboard, Judd steamed off to the passenger deck with a sour puss, while Grant and Damien both stepped onto the *Nighthawk.*

"Damien, I didn't expect you'd come on this trip," Grant said. The deckhands unfastened the heavy chains holding the boat to the ramp and put up the stanchions and safety chains across the open stern. "I thought you just came down to make sure I got all the reservations aboard."

"Really, Grant? We never doubt that you do a good job loading the boat."

"Good to know," Grant said. He held up his portable radio and said, "All set on the stern, Tom."

"To be honest," Grant said to Damien after the deckhands left the stern. "My only problem is Judd. He isn't a good fit for this boat."

"He isn't a good fit for any boat," Damien said. "We put him with you and Tom because you two seem to be able to keep him under control."

"Thanks for nothing," Grant said. By then the engines had come up to speed and the deck under their feet shook and jumped like a minor earthquake as the giant propellers beneath the stern took their first unsteady bites of water. The wash from the propellers sent torrents of whitewater against the back of the slip as the *Nighthawk* pulled out. Grant had known Damien since the younger man was a child who came down to the boats with his father. Roland would sometimes leave the boy with him after saying, "Teach the kid something, Grant." So he knew he was on firm enough footing with Damien.

"The thing is—Judd is a big pussy," Grant said when the boat was under way and the pilings of the slip were speeding by. "When he tries to confront a passenger over some simple problem, he gets nervous and overreacts. Then he starts to sweat—profusely, like all over his face— and then he farts. And his farts are loud—ass cheek slamming loud— and god-awful smelly. Which only makes him more nervous."

"I know, but we can't do anything about that yet," Damien said. "Everybody knows that Judd and some of the other security people are woefully unfit for their jobs, but we have to take whoever the contractor sends us if they are qualified on paper."

"Yet?" Grant said. "What do you mean you can't do anything yet? Are you working on something to get rid of him?"

"Keep this under your hat," Damien said. "We're fairly sure that the security company lied to get the contract. Judd's qualifications are bullshit, and the lawyers are working on a fix to your problem right now."

"Great," Grant said. "It can't happen soon enough." The loading ramp and the pilings of the ferry terminal were disappearing in the fog behind them as the *Nighthawk* steamed out of the channel, with the foghorn sounding like a mighty Viking battle horn, warning all boats that a large vessel needed the fairway. "So why are you coming over to the island, anyway?

"There's a traffic jam slowing things up at our loading dock on the island," Damien said. "Dad wants me to sort out some sort of security snafu—all due to that annual conference of billionaires that's going on next door to our terminal. They try to stay low-key, but I guess somebody figured out that the world's top tech entrepreneurs and the CEOs of the biggest technology companies are all huddled at the Nantucket Yacht Club this weekend."

The Hammerhead

Younger sailors scattered when Master Chief Petty Officer Jack Bramble wheeled his red Caddy convertible onto the pier at the Coast Guard base at Woods Hole—wearing dark sunglasses and a dress hat with two gold stars above a chiefs' anchor—because they all knew that while he might not actually run them down, he would certainly give them an ass-chewing they could tell their grandchildren about if they failed to get out of his way. Likewise, it was well known that the Master Chief's parking spot near the gangway of the Coast Guard Cutter *Hammerhead* had better be clear of all objects and personnel in the morning, because he would not look before pulling in to park his car there.

The patrol boat's engines were already idling when Jack got out of the Caddy and slammed the door shut. "*Hammerhead* arriving!" was announced over the loudspeaker as he came up the gangway, where he chopped a half-salute at the stars and stripes on the stern before tossing his keys at the nearest young deckhand, who nearly fumbled the catch in surprise.

"Put up the top on that fine example of automobile design," Jack said, pointing a thumb over his shoulder at the Caddy.

His chief engineer was standing in the door to the engine room. "We're all set, Jack," Chief Mike Barlow said. "Full fuel and water, and all the machinery is good to go."

"Jeez, Mike, you look like shit," Jack said. "You must have been out hooting with the owls last night."

"What do you expect from a geo?" Mike said. He'd become a geographic bachelor for his tour of duty on the *Hammerhead* rather than move his family up from Virginia while his son and daughter were in high school. "But I'm always ready to soar with the eagles in the morning."

"You and me both," Jack said as he climbed the ladder to the pilothouse, where he was greeted by his new executive petty officer, a young first-class boatswain's mate named Neal Potter.

"Morning, Master Chief," Neal said. He was technically second-in-command of the *Hammerhead*, even though he was a full pay grade below Chief Mike, and far short of Jack in experience and credibility with the crew. He was one of the promising young petty officers that the Coast Guard (in their infinite wisdom, Jack would say) threw head first into a sink-or-swim billet where they might divine the unwritten secrets of success for their own command afloat sometime in the future—or not.

Jack ignored Neal and poured a cup of coffee from the stainless carafe on the chart table. He yelled out the door to the kid with his car keys, "Close the windows too, you damn numbskull."

He pushed his dress hat farther back on his head and took a gulp of the black brew before he looked at Neal and said, "Let's pull the gangway aboard and get the hell out of here, Neal."

Wearing a dress hat with working blues had not been acceptable under the most current uniform regulations for several decades, but junior officers would never dare to correct the master chief on a petty matter, and senior officers—who were almost as old and long-serving—enjoyed giving Jack a pass, since it implied that they, too, were connected to the "old guard" and the way things used to be.

There was not an admiral in the service who was prouder of their stars, or more respected, than a master chief petty officer. Then again, the brass needed men like Jack Bramble to descend on a unit where the new doctrine of kinder-gentler discipline had faltered, and a crew needed an attitude adjustment. Jack had squared away such sticky situations at several small units in recent years with impressive results and little embarrassing publicity, which had earned him command of this brand-new eighty-seven-foot patrol boat, the *Hammerhead*, as his twilight assignment before retirement.

The Marine Protector-class boats—which everyone called Eighty-sevens—were powerful and nimble, with rigid-hull inflatable rescue boats on a stern ramp that could be safely launched and recovered in sloppy seas, as well as two .50 caliber machine guns on the bow. Yet old salts lamented that they were mass-produced fabrications that lacked souls, with hard chines and flat hull plating where the earlier patrol boats—the Eighty-twos and Ninety-fives—had tumble home and graceful curves that were reminiscent of the era of chasing U-boats and playing tag with rumrunners. Perhaps as a reflection of the Coast Guard's split personality since the ascension of the national security mission, half of the Eighty-sevens had been given aggressive names such as *Barracuda*, *Mako*, *Tiger Shark*, and *Diamondback*, while others had gentler names like *Osprey*, *Pelican*, and *Manatee*, which might reflect a longing for the service's humanitarian and lifesaving roots.

"Take her out, Neal," Jack said, pulling off his sunglasses and nodding toward the thick bank of fog that was standing off the Nobska Point Lighthouse at the entrance to the harbor.

"Aye, Master Chief. Take in lines one, two, and four! Hold line three!"

Neal backed on the port shaft to spring the bow out before he said, "Take in line three!" and pointed the *Hammerhead* out of the channel.

"Master Chief," Neal said as they idled past the Nobska Point Lighthouse. "I'm just trying to get settled into this billet as your executive petty officer—so can I ask you something?"

"Shoot."

"Well, it's about your leadership style. I do not get it. You bark and snarl at the crew all day long—and they love you for it. That's not what they taught us at leadership and management school."

"Look, Neal, you could have taken a six-week vacation in Las Vegas instead of going to that school. I'll teach you all you need to know about leadership in six minutes."

"I'm listening, Master Chief."

"Good. Watch this," Jack said, as he leaned out the open side window of the pilothouse and pointed down at a life-rail stanchion on the deck. "Who painted this goddamn stanchion?"

A skinny young seaman-apprentice who was stowing the mooring lines looked up and said, "That was me, Master Chief. Yesterday afternoon I noticed that some rust needed attention."

"Well I'll be," Jack said, with a thumbs-up gesture. "Barnes, you're usually as worthless as a prom date with lockjaw. It is about time you did something useful. Keep it up."

As soon as Jack's head was back inside the pilothouse the other crewmen on deck stifled laughs and silently razzed Barnes, holding their fists to their noses in the international "brownnose" gesture.

"Look out there now," Jack said to Neal. "Tell me what's going on down on the deck plates."

"They picked up the pace stowing those lines," Neal said. "They're sort of having a good time. Barnes is laughing his fool head off."

"Okay, that's lesson one. Pay attention to little details on the boat. When you see something you like, say something in public. When you see something you don't like, say something in private."

"That's easy enough. What else?"

"Neal, I want you to go down and scrub a commode."

"But, Master Chief, I'm the exec on this boat. I shouldn't have to do that,"

"You think I never scrubbed a shitter?"

"Well—"

"Listen, this part is important. It is one thing for them to know you have done all the lousy jobs you tell them to do—but it is something else for them to see it. So, go down and show a new guy the right way to clean a commode sometime. Get it?"

"Loud and clear, Master Chief."

"Okay, now I'll let you in on a little secret. If any crewmember on this boat has a problem, it is my problem too. Whether it's money, family crap, girlfriends, wives, or some bullshit here on the boat. They know that if they come to me, we are going to get them squared away, whatever it takes. They have to know that if they're doing a good job for the boat, that when things get real, you and I are always on their side."

"I like that part, Skipper. But I still do not get how they like being yelled at and abused by you. It is almost like they enjoy it. But I notice that you are sort of smiling when you growl, like you are having a good time, too. So, is it all an act?"

"It's dead serious," the master chief said. "They're my crew and they know damn well that I'll fire a broadside at anybody from off this boat who is dumb enough to give them a ration of shit. You'd better believe I will go to general quarters on any lieutenant or commander that screws with my men. I love that kind of fight. That is why I'll stand toe-to-toe with any officer who says one unfair thing about my crew and chew his head off—what have I got to lose? This is my twilight tour before I retire. But don't you try that, Neal. I want you to do everything calmly and exactly by the book. Let me play the fun part."

"That's a deal, Master Chief."

"Good. One last thing: never be the senior man with a secret. That is my job. I want to know everything you know about what goes on with the crew, on or off the boat, good, bad, and ugly."

"Got it."

When they rounded Nobska Point, one look at the radar confirmed that their course to Nantucket was blocked by a clot of sailboats stumbling blindly in the fog at the entrance to the harbor and the passage into Buzzards Bay. Each blip on the screen projected a dotted line showing its course, speed, and future position as predicted by the computer, and these vectors crossed and competed with each other as boats jockeyed for the best course to steer, without really knowing where they were themselves, much less the other guy.

"That's a nice sword fight," Jack said, laughing at the crossed vectors on the screen.

"We ought to be able to pick our way through this mess if we go slowly," Neal said.

"That's not how I operate," Jack said. He shoved the throttles down and the diesels roared, sending plumes of spray aside as the *Hammerhead* jumped up to full speed. "Didn't you ever go slalom skiing with a boat? Just weave and turn behind everybody."

"Oh boy, we're going to scare the crap out of these blow-boaters, Master Chief," Neal said as he turned the wheel furiously.

"Fuck 'em if they can't take a joke."

The Passenger Deck

The *Nighthawk* was not yet clear of Hyannis Harbor when Grant left the freight deck and climbed the stairs to the passenger deck. The enclosed stairway opened onto a covered promenade under the sundeck that went all around the two large passenger compartments, where a few passengers had stepped outside to smoke. There was plenty of room a short distance away for other passengers who stood by the railing to gaze into the blank wall of fog, which held the tantalizing aromas of shoal water and the sounds of coastal birds.

"Yes, ma'am," he assured one woman in passing. "The fog is not unusual, that's why they call Nantucket the Gray Lady. We expect to arrive at the island on schedule."

"No, sir," he informed a man wearing the ball cap of a Korean War naval veteran. "Ships don't have slow to bare steerageway in fog these days. We have the best radar, and the rules of the road allow us to proceed in near-zero visibility."

He spoke to others who hoped to see the Kennedy Compound as they left the harbor, but he had to inform them that "Camelot" would be well hidden by the fog. Another passenger asked about Great White Sharks, which had been much in the news lately for attacking swimmers on the cape. "We're not likely to see any Great Whites on this crossing," Grant said. "They are mostly on the outer coast of the cape and the islands, where there are lots of seals. But I would be very careful about swimming anywhere around here this time of year."

It was Grant's habit to stroll through the passenger compartments before he reported to the wheelhouse. The atmosphere inside, where most travelers were still getting settled for the crossing, was quite different from the open air of the promenade. The aft compartment was divided into booths with tables, except for thirty-six airline-style seats facing a big-screen television, which was always tuned to a twenty-four-hour New England regional news channel, heavy with coverage of sports and small-town events. Re-tuning the TV to any national news channel was a perilous exercise for the crewman on watch, since the passengers were often equally divided, with strong preferences for, and against, the networks. In a pinch, Grant was not above turning off the satellite antenna, which reverted the screen to a loop of Nantucket Steamboat Company promo videos.

The booths at the rear of the compartment were reserved for passengers with pets, which was where the girl in the plaid skirt was sitting with her Yorkie in her lap. Grant knew that her family would be happy to have her take a flight to their summer home on the island, but the airlines would require her terrier to travel in a cage.

In the booths farther forward, a baby was wailing, and a man was hacking with a wet cough. A grandmother was giving directions to children who really did not need or want her help to select their seat. A lone man in hiking attire, with knee socks and a colorful Nepal knit cap with tassels hanging from the ear flaps, had staked his solo claim to a four-person booth by scattering his backpack, jacket, and notebook all around. A woman with a wicked South Boston accent was loudly recounting some petty house party escapade to her friends and laughing hysterically at her own words, which reached all the ears in the cabin, uninvited.

Grant walked through this assemblage of humanity holding the tickets he had collected on the boarding ramp. He recognized many of the islanders who had made the crossing many times—they almost all sat quietly with a magazine or a book in their lap—and most said hello or silently nodded with recognition as he walked by. Which was why, on the rare occasions when the *Nighthawk* had a layover night on the island, he never had to pay for a beer in any drinking establishment on Nantucket.

A narrow passageway separated the passenger compartments, with restrooms and a storage locker for cleaning supplies on both sides, as well as a large alcove packed with video gaming machines. The ship's documents and the crew's licenses were posted under locked glass on the bulkhead near the game room. The heavy steel fire doors that could isolate the two compartments in an emergency were normally kept open.

The forward passenger compartment was slightly larger, with booths along the windows looking out to the promenade, and airline seating in the center. The kid in the Roger Williams sweatshirt was in one of the single seats with his backpack on the floor between his feet. He was reading a paperback copy of *Catcher in the Rye*. Grant recalled that his name was Arthur and that his family lived above their restaurant on Old North Wharf. He asked him about his plans for the summer even though he knew what the answer would be. "Some of my friends went to Europe," Arthur said. "But I have to work in my family's restaurant. Boy, does that make the summer go fast."

The delicatessen was located near the front of the compartment, with a bulkhead separating it from the kitchen. Grant saw that Damien had taken a small two-person booth near the food service counter, where his notebook and papers were spread on the table. The family that owned the Highland Steamboat Company preferred to remain anonymous when they traveled on their boats, so Grant nodded to Damien as he walked by. When he got close to the food service counter, Katarina motioned for him to come into the kitchen.

"There is a man in the cocktail lounge who worked on this boat for a short time," she said. "I only mention this because he was banned from the property when he left the company—and I am responsible for his dismissal."

"Who is it?" Grant said.

"Zack Brody."

"You're sure it is him?" Grant said. The lounge was at the very front of the passenger spaces, separated from the delicatessen by the kitchen. There was a long settee under large windows on three sides of the space, with small tables and chairs in the center, and the two televisions above the bar were always tuned to sports channels. The front-facing windows offered a grand view ahead of the vessel, but on this crossing only a wall of fog was visible ahead of the mooring bitts and anchor-handling gear on the bow. Grant peeked out the door of the kitchen to catch sight of the man, but his view was blocked by some passengers who were still finding their seats and getting settled.

"Yes," Katarina said. "He was quite lazy and disruptive. His application to work as a deckhand was rejected for some petty crimes he had once committed, but Roland gave him a chance to prove himself behind the deli counter. Unfortunately, Zack believed that cleaning the kitchen and serving customers was beneath his dignity."

"Now I remember that guy," Grant said. "This was two years ago, wasn't it? I could not see his face under the brim of his cap when he came aboard, but I should have recognized the tattoos on his neck. He was sleeping—or pretending to sleep—in the cab of a Boston catering truck."

I should have noticed the tattoos, Grant thought. If only Judd was not bothering that woman behind my back.

"Yes, those tattoos—he tried to keep them hidden at first—but they were disgusting. One day he tried to frighten us girls by unbuttoning his shirt and showing us the Nazi slogans and symbols on his chest, but that was only part of his undoing. A few days later I caught him standing under the stairs while the boat was loading on Nantucket. He was pretending to talk on his cell phone, but it was obvious that he was up-skirting women on the stairs with his phone's camera. Roland was waiting on the dock when we pulled into Hyannis, and he personally removed him from the boat, quite forcefully, with instruction to never return."

"Right," Grant said. "I remember that. But I have to say, even though he was banned from loitering on the property, we can't refuse him if he buys a ticket for the crossing."

"So, we can't go back to the dock and put him off?"

"No," Grant said, laughing at the suggestion. "How about this—should I make him walk the plank halfway to Nantucket?"

"Seriously, Grant, that man is dangerous. I have often worried that he is going to step out of the shadows and harm me."

"We won't let that happen, Katarina. I will tell Tony to keep an eye on him. You should give the wheelhouse a call if he comes near the delicatessen. Tom will send someone right down here."

"And what about Judd? Isn't this a matter for the security man?"

"You may have to call Judd if Zack comes near you or the deli," Grant said. "But if he stays in his seat and behaves himself, let us leave Judd out of it, because our security man has a habit of provoking people. If it comes to it, you can always hit the trouble button under the counter. Don't worry, the rest of us will have your back."

"Thank you," Katarina said, with a knowing smile. "That is what I needed to hear."

2

SOULS ONBOARD

The Galley

While Grant loaded the boat in Hyannis, Justin Boudreaux was preparing a roast and gumbo for the crew's lunch. His galley was on the sundeck—the uppermost level of the boat—along with the crews' quarters and the wheelhouse, behind doors that denied entry to all passengers. Which was fine with the cook. Working on the boats for decades had left him with little patience for foolish questions and idle comments. He was a tall, slope-shouldered man with heavy bones, prone to somewhat ponderous movements, as if he were always exhausted. He wore a white apron folded at his beltline over dungarees and a tee shirt that was clean at the start of each day, and he kept the fingernails on his pinkies long to more easily peel the skins off garlic, an ingredient he used in abundance. When he felt the deck vibrate as the diesel engines started four decks below, he knew that the crew would be streaming through his galley as soon as they tossed off the mooring lines and chains, so he got the teakettle steaming and set a tray of cinnamon rolls, fresh out of his oven.

Dana McSorley had the helm watch, so she came through first, ponytail trailing, and her tanned legs in shorts stepping lively. Justin thought that the galley was not quite so drab when she came in to make her tea. The crew seemed to love having her onboard just for the way she smiled and laughed at their ill manners and crude language—as long as none of it was directed at her—but it was the fact that she could work on deck as hard and fast as any man, without making a big deal out of it, that made her something special.

"How's that roast coming?" Dana said.

"It'll be ready when we get to Nantucket," Justin said, speaking slowly with an accent that was straight out of the French Quarter.

"What temperature do you cook it at?"

"Now, don't be that way," Justin said. "I don't tell you how to steer the boat, do I?"

Todd Bell was a cadet at the Massachusetts Maritime Academy who homed in on the sweet aroma of the cinnamon rolls as soon as the door to the galley opened. He wore blue shorts like Dana, while the older deckhands all wore long trousers. Todd was working on the *Nighthawk* for the summer, a slim nineteen-year-old with a copy of *Eldridge's* tide and pilot book tucked into his belt at the small of his back, full of youthful energy that might explode into manhood at any moment—perhaps even as he began pulling one of the plump rolls apart with gusto.

"Hey, Todd," Tony said. The muscleman stuttered slightly when excited. "You're going to leave some of those for the rest of us, right?" Tony DeLuca was a lean bodybuilder who reminded everyone of the late Jack LaLanne, who with his form-fitting jumpsuits and wide-legged stance had been the prototype of the television fitness guru. Sometimes, in fact, passengers of a certain age thought Tony might be the son of the legendary Hollywood bodybuilder who had fallen on hard times and taken a job on the boats.

Dana was making a cup of Earl Grey tea and Todd had spooned some cocoa mix into a mug after he inhaled half the roll. He was standing close behind her in line for the teakettle when he said, "Hey, Dana, do you want some honey for your tea?"

"No thanks, Todd. I can get it off the counter myself."

"How about half of this cinnamon roll? It's still warm from the oven."

"I definitely don't want a half-eaten cinnamon bun, Todd."

"Okay," Todd said. "I just wanted to say thanks for this tide and pilot book. There's a lot of cool stuff in here."

"No problem, Todd. I do not need it anymore, and this way you don't have to pester me with so many questions. It's all in the book."

So, I've been wondering," Todd said, going ahead with a question, nevertheless. "Why do you carry a knife in the middle of your back?"

"So that I can reach it with either hand when I'm climbing in the rigging."

"There's no rigging on this boat."

"I've mostly worked on tall ships," she said. "This job is—temporary."

"Why don't you work on tall ships anymore?"

"Oh boy," Justin said, shaking his head and smashing a clove of garlic with a cleaver.

"Jeez, Todd," Tony muttered. "Don't—"

Dana turned around and said, "Stop gawking at my butt, Todd."

"I wasn't," Todd said, stammering. "I just saw that you carried the knife there, and—"

"Why not?" Tony said. "What's wrong with her butt? I look at her tail all the time. Don't you like girls?"

Todd said, "She's not a girl—I mean, she is a girl—but she's one of the crew. So—"

"Sounds like somebody has a little crush on you, Dana," Justin said.

Grant had come into the galley in the middle of this and he said, "Just stop talking, Todd. You are only digging a deeper hole for yourself. Grab your hot chocolate and another cinnamon bun and get out of here."

"Gee, I'm sorry," Todd said, and the galley erupted into laughter after he was off.

"Dana, stop being mean to that kid," Grant said.

"He's an awesome kid," Dana said as she headed to the wheelhouse. "I just like to screw with him. Did you see the way his peach-fuzz cheeks turn red?"

"Sure, but he doesn't know why you don't work under sail anymore."

"Maybe one of you ought to tell him," Justin said, smashing a clove of garlic under his cleaver.

The Delicatessen

Damien knew that Justin would be happy to feed him and tell him a new joke if he went up another flight of stairs to the galley. But the off-watch crew would soon be playing cards at their long mess table and it was always awkward for one of the owners to walk in on them during their break. Nor would he take a seat in the wheelhouse with Captain Tom since the presence of an owner might be a distraction when the vessel was navigating in fog. So, Damien had settled into an isolated booth in the forward passenger space, across from the delicatessen, where he could spread out the previous month's manifests and receipts in relative privacy. He nodded at Grant when he passed through and went behind the food service counter for some issue, and later he saw Tony DeLuca come into the passenger cabin and start making his rounds, taking the time to talk to the customers.

He could also see Katarina, but she gave her undivided attention to the customers standing at the snack bar. Damien recognized one of them as the man who came aboard last with his family in a minivan, and he was close enough to see that there was a police badge in the man's wallet when he paid for two coffees and left a nice tip in Katarina's jar.

Then the svelte blonde behind the counter glanced at him while serving the last person in line.

Did she just smile at me? Damien thought. As in, come here? He waited a minute before he stood up to the snack bar and said, "I'll have a coffee."

"Here you are, sir," Katarina said after she added cream and sugar.

"Thanks."

"Are you enjoying the trip, sir?"

Damien leaned across the counter and he said, "What's with the 'sir' stuff?"

"It's a necessary part of this little masquerade we're playing, isn't it?"

"Not now," Damien said. He took his coffee back to his seat and shuffled the papers. *Why do her eyes have to be so damn blue*, he thought?

A deeper blue than any others he had ever seen. When he looked her way again, she raised her pretty little nose as she turned away—*the hell with you*—and went into the storeroom. The other girls working behind the snack bar scattered when Damien followed her into the tiny space of the kitchen storeroom, where he said, "Kat, please don't do this."

"Have I offended you, sir?"

"For Christ sake, stop calling me 'sir' after every sentence."

"Perhaps for appearances I should treat you the same as any other customer on the boat?"

"Just cut out the 'sir' crap, okay? We can be cordial, at least."

"Is that your command as my employer, or—?"

"Damn it, this isn't the time or place for this."

"You're right," she said. "So, go back to your seat."

"We'll talk later."

"Or not," she said.

"What does that mean?"

"It means you can't invite me to your bed and then ignore me on your boat."

"My family—"

"Yes, your family. I am sure they will be elated when my work visa expires and I must return home."

"I told you—we'll meet in Paris."

"When?"

"As soon as I can get free."

"I may be foolish—but I do believe you, Damien," she said as she leaned in to touch his chest. "But if we are to remain intimate all I ask for is a slight deference—you can't ignore me in front of the other girls in my workplace. Do not worry, they will not expose us. We girls from the Balkans know which secrets must be kept."

The Freight Deck

When Grant left the galley, he went down to the freight deck and stood at the stern, where the *Nighthawk*'s massive unseen propellers churned the gray water of Nantucket Sound into a quicksilver boil trailing the hull. He knew they were clear of the channel because Tom had brought the engines up to speed, causing the steel deck under his feet to vibrate in the shallow water west of Bishop and Clerks Rocks. He lit his third—fourth?—cigarette of the day and stood briefly at the chains and looked across the transom to where the boat's wake disappeared into the fog, pondering the number of times that he had made this exact crossing between Hyannis and Nantucket.

Every trip was different, the old-timers would say. The tide and wind were never the same, there was constantly a new crop of passengers, and every landing against a ramp with the big boats was another chance to excel.

Anyway, that's what they'd say.

He did not have to wait long for Todd to come walking toward the stern between the rows of cars and trucks to stand at his side.

"What's up?" Todd said.

"I need to talk to you about Dana," Grant said. When he turned toward the youngster, he could feel the heat of the big diesels coming up from the shadows inside the open door to the engine room, in an alcove about thirty feet away.

"Yeah, I can't figure her out," Todd said. "She's tough, but she's always teaching me useful things." He held up a small book with a yellow cover for Grant to see. "Sometimes she's real nice to me. Last week she gave me this copy of *Eldridge's* tide and pilot book that she did not need anymore. Then I try to be nice to her today—but I always say the wrong thing."

"You don't say the wrong thing to Justin, or Tony, or me. So, what do you think?"

"I don't usually have trouble talking to girls. Honest, Grant—I don't."

"She's not a girl, Todd. She is a woman. An extremely attractive, smart woman."

"I know she's out of my league," Todd said. "I just—"

"I wouldn't say that, Todd. She is older, that's all. And she has a life off the boat that you don't know anything about."

"Yeah, but we still have to work together. I mean—"

"All right, here it is," Grant said. "You hit on her sore spot. Before she worked here Dana was the first mate on the *Calliope*."

"Isn't that the sailing ship that sank in a hurricane last year? So, she was shipwrecked?"

"No, she wasn't aboard the ship for the disaster because she fell from the mainmast a few weeks earlier and screwed up her shoulder. She was at home recovering from some broken bones while a younger crewmember with much less experience was acting as mate for that voyage. They were taking the ship down to the Caribbean for the winter."

"Then it sounds like she was lucky to miss the storm."

"Not really, Todd. If Dana were working on the *Calliope* for that voyage—the way she sees it—the ship would not have been lost. The kid who replaced her did not have the backbone to stand up to the reckless captain. That ship looked seaworthy, but it was designed as a movie prop that was used to carry tourists around Buzzards Bay on sunny afternoons. If Dana had been aboard, she never would have allowed the captain to sail that leaky old barge straight into a hurricane."

"Gee, Grant, I didn't know. At least she didn't drown."

"No, but many of her shipmates were lost—which might be worse."

"Golly, after that, I'd never want to work on a boat again."

"It's the money, Todd. And pride. Working on the water is all she knows how to do. She had to work her butt off and take a lot of gruff to get her license. I will tell you a little secret, too—her shoulder is all healed. Fact is that any sailing ship would be happy to have her as mate. Except that after her fall—and the loss of her shipmates—her confidence is gone. She is too terrified of heights to climb in the rigging. That's why she's working here."

Todd paused and looked at the deck for a moment before he said, "Why didn't somebody tell me?"

"You didn't ask," Grant said, putting a hand on Todd's shoulder. "Give her a little space, Todd. That *Eldridge's* book is full of practical information you might not find in your textbooks. Maybe she gave it to you because you're the maritime cadet who reminds her of another young shipmate—a kid who had all the right answers on the mate's examination—but not enough sea-sense to steer clear of a storm."

The Aft Passenger Compartment

Sean Lamont was pleased by what he did not see while carrying two cups of coffee through the passenger spaces on the ferry *Nighthawk*. Walking past the booths and tables near the delicatessen, through the narrow passageway between the restrooms, and into the large aft compartment full of people, he did not see any of the purse-snatchers, pickpockets, strong-arm goons, or armed robbers that were his constant targets in the Manhattan South Patrol Bureau of the New York City Police Department.

When he was on the job, Sergeant Lamont was the leader of a small team of hard-charging cops that patrolled in plainclothes and nondescript vehicles. They wore regulation gun-belts under civilian shirts or jackets with their shields on silver chains around their necks. Their job was to blend with the populace to spot trouble and spring into action before the 9-1-1 call. Perhaps because his father and grandfather had worked the streets of New York, Sean had an instinct for spotting nascent criminal acts. He knew how perps walked to case their mark and plan their escape route, and the haughty way they carried themselves in the moments before the crime, when they cornered a weaker opponent in a doorway, or an alley, or strode into a storefront with a stolen handgun, and felt powerful and in charge.

Sean's job was to blunt that haughtiness and ruin their day—but not this day.

On this day Sean was taking his family to Nantucket for their first real family vacation. He and Helen had enjoyed romantic getaways to Mexico, the Virgin Islands, and Jamaica before the twins were born, and lately they had sometimes managed to get away from the city for a weekend. This would be their first full week in a rented cottage on the island with the boys and Olivia, who was just taking her first steps.

In passing, he took a good look at the five rough-looking men who occupied a row of seats facing a large-screen television mounted to the wall behind the restrooms. They sported dark beards, and their clothes were Carhartt and Gander Mountain, with a smattering of tattered foreign military items. Except for one giant of a man in a dirty white t-shirt and bib coveralls, whose white hair and beard coalesced into a singular mop that fell over his shoulders and down to his ample stomach. There were a few patches and tattoos that gave Sean pause, but he pretended not to notice and kept walking past them to the booth at the back of the compartment where Helen was sticking straws into juice boxes.

She was wearing her sandy blonde hair shorter now—three young children did not leave her much time for hair maintenance—but she still made a point of playing tennis three times each week. Helen had always been a pretty girl, but there were lots of pretty girls in the Borough of Queens. It was her natural athleticism that closed the deal on their marriage, when it was added to the clear-thinking brain and zest for life that she would pass on to their children. Not that he had weighed all those factors prior to their nuptials—does any man?—Helen had always been the neighborhood girl who got him hard.

"Push in so I can sit next to you," Sean said, when he reached their table.

"What is it?"

"I just want to keep an eye on something," he said. The new seating arrangement allowed him to see the five men as he cut an apple with his pocketknife and handed the slices to the children. Richard and Theodore were identical twins, five years old. Although Teddy seldom missed an opportunity to assert that he had come into the world twenty minutes ahead of his brother. Sitting across the table from them, Sean proudly noticed—for the umpteenth time—that their New York Mets sweatshirts fit nicely over their shoulders, which were already broad, straight, and square. When Olivia smiled at him while hanging on to Helen with one hand and daintily nibbling her slice of apple in her mother's lap, he felt like the luckiest man in the world.

"I hope the captain can find Nantucket in the fog," Teddy said, between bites of apple. He was sitting next to the window at their table, where only gray mist was visible beyond the promenade.

"Don't be stupid," Ricky said. "He's got sonar."

"Radar," their father said.

A crewmember was making rounds of the passenger deck and when he came to their table and said, "Are you folks enjoying the trip?"

"Everything is fine," Helen said. "Thank you."

"Right," Sean said. "Do people ever tell you that you that you look like Jack LaLanne?"

"All the time," the crewman said, swelling with pride and flexing into a strongman stance. "There's no relation, though. At least not that I know of."

"Okay, Mister Muscleman," Sean said, pointing with his chin. "What do you think of those five guys over there in front of the television?"

"Not much. I have seen them on here before, so they must be contractors or the crew of a fishing boat or something. They pretty much keep to themselves."

"Thanks."

"Do you feel better now?" Helen said after the crewman continued his rounds. "Maybe you could stop being a cop for the rest of the week?"

"Sure," Sean said. He rolled an orange on the tabletop and peeled the rind away with the knife to hand slices to his children while watching the five men on the far side of the cabin.

On the job, real working men were a cop's best friend. Sean remembered one time when he was a rookie chasing a purse-snatcher into an alley, where he got into a struggle with the perp and two of his accomplices. It was touch-and-go until a group of construction workers from across the street streamed into the alley and evened the score.

Yet there was something about these five. First, their hands did not look hard enough, and their clothes did not have a single union or tool logo. Moreover, the emblems they did display were ominous—some would say threatening.

The yellow "Don't tread on me" Gadsden patches with a rattlesnake coiled to strike might be a benign libertarian statement, or just a cool ornament available in any novelty shop. Yet he had noticed that one of the men wore a patch with the number "14" on his shoulder, while another's sleeve was rolled up to expose a crude tattoo of a squared-off

Celtic cross in a circle. Sean had seen these symbols posted on the bulletin board in his precinct house, along with the latest prison gang identifiers. The "14" referenced the fourteen words of a white supremacist slogan: "We must secure the existence of our people and a future for white children." The squared Celtic cross intersecting a circle could be an even more virulent sign of neo-Nazi sentiments.

Whatever, Sean finally decided, it did not matter. If these guys had been on the boat before, they were probably going to the island to do another shabby job, for which they would overcharge some unfortunate homeowner, and then be gone. The antisocial signals these men were transmitting were probably under the radar of island residents and tourists, who were content and oblivious in their affluent paradise. Hopefully, the local constabulary, at least, would recognize that drug abuse, petty crime, and violent racism traveled with these symbols.

If they were up to no good, that would be a problem for the cops on the island. Nantucket was two hundred miles from Manhattan. And unfortunately, Sean's Glock pistol with twelve rounds of 9mm ammunition in the magazine was one deck below, under the driver's seat of the family minivan at the back of the boat.

3

MEN'S LIVES

The dragger Nova Sintra

Captain Geno Branca was a crusty little man with powerful hands, alone in the wheelhouse of a small wooden boat on the edge of a great sea, surrounded by fog. This was the fishing vessel *Nova Sintra,* a seventy-two-foot western-rig dragger out of New Bedford, with a reel of nets on the stern, a pilothouse with a galley forward, and a high pitched bow for cutting through the steep seas that roam freely on George's Bank.

Geno leaned close to the radar screen to study the blurred image as he approached Nantucket Harbor, where the rock jetties on both sides of the narrow channel looked like the maw of a monster fish poised to clamp down on him. He much preferred the open water on Asia Rip, Rose and Crown, or Davis Bank, where he could tow his nets for hours in any direction. In fact, he had no desire to leave the fishing grounds and go into a harbor that was fifty miles away from his homeport— except that two of his crewmen were cowering in their bunks, both bleeding from gashes on their heads.

"I'll tell you, these *beberrãos* aren't real fishermen," Geno said, speaking into the radio microphone in his hand. "In the old days—you know yourself—back in the day you got up from your deathbed to work on deck, right? I know guys who hauled nets with broken arms, guys had their skulls cracked open on the first set and kept on working the rest of the trip. You know yourself, there are no real fishermen left. A snatch-block on the gallows gives way and hits two of my guys in the head—two guys!—half my crew—what kind of shit is that? Half my crew is standing in the wrong damn place at the same damn time, no matter how many times I yelled at them for that stupid shit. I could stitch them up myself in two minutes—but no—they must have a doctor sew up the little cuts on their skulls. But I'll swallow the frog—I'll take them to a damn doctor on the island—and if I can find two fellas who can stand up, I'll hire them both right off the dock, and my bums can damn well swim back to New *Beige*, for all I care."

Geno was talking to his second cousin on the scallop dragger *Lady of Fatima*, but in a larger sense he was contributing to the constant stream of words that fishermen offered to one another on certain marine radio channels, all day and all night. Often this electronic chatter carried whistles, grunts, and cryptic phrases that the captains used to communicate with friends and confuse the uninitiated, like pods of whales navigating the vast open sea with cetaceous sonar—a click of the tongue and a sigh of resignation might really mean, "we're onto big schools of cod over here"—but mostly the captains listened in on the constant radio verbiage and scratchy static to stay awake and share the misery of their disappearing way of life.

"Okay, I got to go over to the other frequency now and listen up," Geno said. "Ha! It would not be good to meet some big ferry coming out of the jetties in this fog, right? See you on the other side."

Geno switched his radio to listen for the ferries, which would make constant announcements on the marine bands as they got under way to proceed outbound from the harbor. But both channel thirteen and channel sixteen on his radio were silent. So, he turned inbound and jimmied the throttle back and ahead slightly to goose the engine twice, which would send spasms through the hull and signal the crew to come up on deck.

Jorge Costa—Geno's trusty mate, engineer, and cook—appeared at his side moments later. "Stinking fog," he said, when he saw that the gray mist was hiding the island. Jorge stayed busy on the boat and didn't speak much. Geno's standard joke was that Jorge would not say shit if he had a mouthful of it. He loved his family and he was a good man.

"Are those bums coming up?" Geno said. "What do they think, we're going to tie the boat up ourselves and carry them off the boat?"

"*Idiotas*," Jorge said, under his breath. By then the *Nova Sintra* was well into the entrance channel. The men did not see the jetties and only knew the rocks were there by the radar. They were more than halfway through the narrow passage when Jorge pointed at the radar and said, "There."

"Where?" Geno said. "That's a house on the point—oh, no. Wait a minute—that is a boat, coming around the point—fast."

Something large was moving behind the lighthouse at Brandt Point, which guarded the entrance to Nantucket Harbor on a narrow peninsula that jutted into the deep-water channel.

"He's really moving," Jorge said.

"Son of a bitch," Geno said, watching a large radar blip swing wide around the point. "What is he doing? The tide is ebbing like a bitch—doesn't he know you can't race the current?"

. "Like an icy road," Jorge said. "No control with the tide up your ass."

Geno pulled the throttle back to idle to slow the *Nova Sintra* to bare steerageway and edged to starboard, hugging his side of the channel.

"*Nova Sintra* calling the boat outbound at Nantucket," Geno said into the radio. "We're coming in the channel. One whistle captain, one whistle."

There was only radio silence from the radar contact that was careening toward them.

"Over there?" Jorge said, pointing his thumb at the other side of the channel. Both men knew that the large vessel coming toward them would have trouble making the turn. With the current behind him he would go wide, no doubt about it.

"Too late," Geno said. "We'll get cut in half if we try to cross his bow. Who is this guy?"

"Look!" Jorge said when the clipper bow of a giant motor yacht came out of the fog, pointed directly at them. Whoever was behind the mirrored glass of the yacht's wheelhouse must have seen the *Nova Sintra* at the same time since they sounded five quick blasts of a powerful air horn.

"*Idiota*," Jorge said. "Wrong side of the channel, and he's blowing at us to get out of his way!"

"*Foda-se!*" Geno said as he spun the wheel in a desperate bid to run his vessel aground in the mud on the right side of the channel if necessary. "Shove the throttle into the corner, Jorge!"

Nova Sintra's GM diesel engine did not hesitate when Jorge slammed the throttle down. She was always a good boat. She jumped into the desperate turn from a standing start, with the sharp bow of the yacht bearing down on her midsection.

Incredibly, Geno's quick action almost got them clear of the giant yacht. But the smaller boat jerked to a sudden stop, then turned sharply and moved backward and sidewise out of control. Both men knew instantly what had happened. The yacht's clipper bow had snagged the *Nova Sintra*'s gallows—the gantry of steel I-beams used to set the nets over the stern—and the smaller boat was being towed backward, sideways, and rolled over. She was being violently capsized.

The pilothouse windows all blew out when the *Nova Sintra* turned upside down and the inrush of seawater was like the spin cycle of a washing machine. Peter the Apostle, patron saint of fishermen, must have pulled Geno and Jorge clear of the wreck because neither man knew how they ended up treading water, watching the yacht slip past them. There was a helicopter on the stern of the gleaming vessel as it continued out of the channel and disappeared into the fog, with the horn still sounding a series of five-blast danger signals. Later, the fishermen would learn that the mega-yacht's owner had insisted on calling his attorney before allowing the captain to notify the Coast Guard of the "mishap" on the boat's satellite telephone.

"Geno, I can't swim."

"Me neither," Geno said, spitting seawater and pointing to the jetty. "But we got to get over there or we are going to drown, so keep kicking, Jorge. Keep kicking with me."

Somehow the two fishermen made it to shallow water alongside the jetty where they could stand up. The bow of the *Nova Sintra* was still partially afloat—though capsized—in the middle of the channel, where the yacht had towed it. Geno and Jorge yelled for the two men who had been below in their bunks but got no answer.

Jorge said, "Too bad they didn't go down like men—with their sea boots on."

Geno saw that fish and ice had spilled from the *Nova Sintra*'s hold and was now floating like a skirt around them.

"My fish," Geno said, holding an iced cod he had picked from the water. "Our last catch, Jorge—we lost it—and two men—it's all over."

"They might be alive in there," Jorge said.

"*Filho de puta*," Geno said, tossing the fish back into the water. "My fish know how to get out of a sinking boat, but my crew don't. Son of a bitch!"

The Hammerhead

Jack was resting his eyes in the pilothouse while Neal navigated the *Hammerhead* eastward across Nantucket Sound toward Great Round Shoals for their week of patrol duty. He muttered "that's bullshit" without opening his eyes when the OPCEN's initial communication with the *Nighthawk* came over the radio, with no explanation for the closing of Nantucket Harbor. But he sat up and raised the brim on his hat when the OPCEN called his unit on the secure communications radio.

"*Hammerhead* proceed to Nantucket Harbor," the radio voice said. Only other government vessels with the daily codes loaded into their radios could hear these transmissions. "A collision in the entrance channel has been reported. The captain of the port has closed the channel to all traffic until the situation is evaluated. The Coast Guard Cutter *Cuttyhunk* is in Nantucket harbor on a priority mission. They will assume on scene commander, report directly to them. Secure communication discipline should be maintained until further notice."

"You've got to be shitting me," Jack said. He jumped out of his seat. "Give me that god-damn microphone."

Jack pushed the button on the microphone to transmit on the secure radio. He said, "OPCEN, what are you telling us? You are a little light on the facts. Did a collision occur, or not? What type of vessels are involved? How many people?"

"*Hammerhead*, at the present time all we have is an initial report," the OPCEN said. "You will investigate and report to the Coast Guard Cutter *Cuttyhunk*. Nothing further, OPCEN out."

"Nothing further, my ass!" Jack said into the radio. "I'm not done talking to you. Why the secrecy? If a Coast Guard vessel is in Nantucket Harbor right now, why aren't they investigating?"

"Negative," the OPCEN said. "The *Cuttyhunk* cannot be diverted from the VIP security zone at this time. Our primary concern is that the channel may be blocked. Proceed to the scene to investigate and maintain the secure communications discipline."

Jack lowered the microphone and scratched his freckled forehead. He looked at his second-in-command, and said, "I don't know, Neal. Did the OPCEN just tell us they don't really care if vessels and people are in distress, because they have a more important security mission two miles away?"

"Heck if I know," Neal said. "Maybe they think the collision is a false report, or a diversion of some kind. A lot of people are all freaked out about the conference this year."

"I don't know why," Jack said. "It's just a bunch of tech geeks having a circle jerk in a back room at the yacht club, getting off about computers and The Cloud, whatever the hell that is. Sounds boring as shit to me." He turned to the quartermaster—Jack called him "Spokes" since the symbol of his rating was an old-fashioned spoked ship's wheel. "Spokes," Jack said, "what's the course to Nantucket Harbor?"

"I make it one-two-zero degrees, Skipper," the young navigator at the chart table said. "That would cut between Norton Shoal and Cross Rip. We can cut the corner at Tuckernuck Shoal too, and shave a few more minutes off."

"Let's roll," Jack said. Neal turned the wheel and pushed the throttles forward. Spray flew from the boat's bow as they rocketed through the fog.

"I don't know what this outfit is coming to," Jack said. "There's nothing I love more than a good search-and-rescue mission. But Christ almighty, I never heard of a top-secret rescue case."

"Search and rescue isn't what it used to be, Master Chief," Neal said. "We're all about national security now."

"Bullshit," Jack said. "Don't you see what's happening here? The *Cuttyhunk* is on a glory mission. They don't want to get called off for some mariners in distress because they're trying to decide where all the medals and awards for a VIP protection mission will go on their dress whites."

"That's harsh, Master Chief," Neal said. "The OPCEN has the big picture. We all have to get onboard with their new mission requirements."

Jack shook his head and said nothing for a few seconds.

Oh no, Neal thought, when Jack raised the radio microphone again. *The master chief is pissed, and the OPCEN is about to get a Flash Priority message from the Old Guard. This is going to be epic.*

"This is Master Chief Bramble," Jack said into the radio. "Who am I talking to in that puzzle palace?"

A new voice came over the radio and said, "This is the Captain of the Port."

"Good, you're exactly the one I want to talk to," Jack said. "W-T-F, Captain, you're not even telling the ferries why the channel is closed. With all due respect—please get your head out of your ass. It will take me thirty-four minutes to get on scene. That is unacceptable if vessels are in distress and other units are closer, sir."

There was long silence before another voice came on the radio. "Your last transmission was garbled and unreadable," said someone who was not the Captain of the Port. "Negative further, OPCEN out."

Jack handed the microphone to Neal and looked at the radar screen and then out to the fog around them. He shook his head, and said, "Neal, I don't think I can keep my head above water in the New Guard anymore. Pass the word to break out all the rescue gear we have. Get ready to tow a disabled vessel, dewater a boat, fight a fire, and—God forbid—rescue people in the water. The whole show. You know what to do. I'll be right back."

"Master Chief, are you okay?"

"I'm fine," Jack said. He turned to go down the ladder to his quarters. "I'm just going below to give birth to an ensign. Then I'll be in my stateroom drafting my retirement letter."

4

THE TURN

The Galley

Not long after Dana, Tony, and Todd went to their stations for the crossing, the off watch came into Justin's galley and took seats at the long table. Without a word of agreement to play, someone produced a cribbage board and a deck of fifty-two dog-eared playing cards. The pegboard was an ancient piece of mahogany trim that had been removed when they remodeled the wheelhouse, with three scrimshaw pegs. A barn-burner matchstick substituted for the fourth peg, which had been lost several seasons and a thousand crossings earlier.

Justin was cleaning a pot in the deep sink while he sized up the competition—they were all lightweights—before he took a seat at the table.

"Dylan, do you want in on this?" Justin said to the third deckhand, who was reading a book on World War Two history at the far end of the table. He was a voracious reader, and at twenty-seven years of age, the youngest man in the galley at that moment. He had left college six years ago to take a job on the boats so his family could keep their land in Harwich. He still intended to go to law school someday.

"No thanks, Justin. I want to finish this book."

"It ends with the Japs getting nuked," the assistant engineer said as he dealt the cards.

"That's too bad, Dylan," Justin said as he sat at the table and opened a spiral notebook. "I like taking money from college boys."

The notebook contained a scribbled record of Justin's winnings, which totaled into the hundreds of dollars—at a penny a point—and which no one would ever pay even if asked to make good on the wagers. Whenever a notebook was full, he would just start a new one with all debts canceled.

The players were mostly men across the threshold of middle age. Except for Lou, who was older, wiry, and weathered, from decades of commercial fishing before he came to the ferries for the steady work and a good health insurance plan. His natural state was a muttering funk. Except that his eyes sometimes lit up when he smiled and laughed so you knew that there was love of life under that grumpy exterior. Then there was St. Pierre, a gentle giant of a man with red hair and a quick smile whom everyone called Saint. The assistant engineer was a fleshy man named Bernard, but he had been called Butch for so many years that even he himself hardly ever used his given name.

These men were all long-term survivors in the marine trades. The summer hires often wondered why these old-timers hustled to handle the mooring lines and chains with dispatch, and why they placed themselves in the most difficult positions when guiding cars and trucks to their parking assignments, where the risk of damage to customers' cars was the most critical. These veteran deckhands saw a job that had to be done and jumped to work. They swung brooms and mops like energized jitterbug dancers and took their turns scrubbing commodes in the passenger bathrooms like turbocharged janitors, leaving the summer hires in their wakes. Then, when the end-of-season layoffs came after Thanksgiving—just before the Christmas bonuses—these men still had secure employment and health insurance for their families while the summer hires were on the street filing for state benefits.

The pegs were making progress up the cribbage board—accompanied by equal parts of laughter and grousing—when Judd came into the galley and scooped a cup of gumbo from the pot on Justin's stove. He maneuvered his bulk past the players, in his shooting vest and amber glasses, and took a seat across from Dylan at the far end of the table.

"The gumbo isn't done yet," Justin said, looking at his cards and not at Judd.

"It's hot enough," Judd said.

"Hot don't mean done," Justin said. "You can't just take food off my stove without asking."

"You want me to put it back?"

The players said, "No," in unison.

"Don't you get tired of sitting on your ass all day?" Lou said.

"I do my job," Judd said.

"When?" Butch said. "I've never seen you lift a finger to help anyone."

"I checked out the passengers as they came aboard," Judd said. "The only suspect was some Arab woman and if she's got a bomb under her robe that's the mate's problem, since he let her on before I could finish questioning her."

"We don't think of them as passengers," Saint said. "They're customers—we do more than give them a ride across Nantucket Sound. We provide a service."

Judd shrugged, which drew a sharp response from Lou.

"You were standing right next to that old lady who was struggling up the stairs with a suitcase," Lou said. "I had to sprint halfway across the freight deck to get to her."

"Whatever," Judd said. "You just wanted the tip. I saw her hand you something at the top of the stairs."

Lou was coming out of his seat when he said, "That's right, Judd. Do you know what she gave me? A quarter—a goddamn quarter—and I smiled and thanked her for it, not because I needed the twenty-five cents, but because it made her feel better to say, 'Thank you, young man.'"

The old fisherman had a lithe physique that was not unlike the knurled branches of a coastal tree that had risen out of a rock crevasse to somehow attain old age in the full force of ocean gales and salt spray, the strength of which fools failed to recognize—and a quiet intensity that younger and larger men disregarded at their own peril.

"It's all about being nice to people," Lou said. "We want them to enjoy the trip and keep coming back. Don't you get that? There are other boats that run to Nantucket, you know."

"I'm not here to pamper these people," Judd said, standing and opening his vest to show off the big .44 Magnum he carried in a shoulder holster. His face was red and beads of sweat seemed to form on his forehead instantly, as if a switch had been thrown. "You'll see how I handle my business when there's trouble on this boat."

"Damn, Judd," Justin said. "Don't you go flashing your gun or your little needle dick in my galley. Why do you need a .44 Magnum, anyway? Who do you think you are, Dirty Harry?"

"Right," Dylan said. "What are you compensating for, Judd?"

"There's no second-place winner in a shoot-out," Judd said.

The crew all laughed, which irritated Judd.

"Just what are your qualifications to carry that cannon?" Butch said. "We're all wondering."

"I didn't know they gave you one of those when you bomb out of the police academy," Dylan said, not looking up from his book.

"Listen, Judd," Saint said. "If you go down there and kick a hornet's nest by pissing off some passengers, don't expect any help from us. You're on your own."

"I don't need this shit from a bunch of deckhands," Judd said. Then he farted when he reached for the handle on the heavy door to the sundeck—a long, sputtering ripper—that drew a chorus of disgust from the players.

"That's okay," Justin said as Judd left them. "Just walk away from your dirty cup and spoon on the table. I'll take it to the sink and clean it later."

"Deckhands," Saint said. "He said the word like we were lower than whale shit."

"He doesn't know shit about boats," Lou said.

They played a few more hands before Lou said, "Hey, do you feel that? We're turning."

"Tom is probably avoiding a lobster boat or something," Butch said.

"No," Saint said, glancing out the window where there was nothing but fog. "It feels like a big turn."

When the sound-powered phone on the bulkhead growled, Justin laid his cards down and reached for the handset.

"Don't worry, Justin," Butch said. "I'll play this hand for you."

"The hell you will," Justin said as he snatched the cards off the table.

"Okay, Cap," Justin said into the phone. Then he sat down and said, "Tommy says we're going back to Hyannis."

"What?"

"Are we going to make the next trip?"

"Will they put another boat on the line?"

"All I want to know is—are we going to get a full day's pay out of this?"

The Aft Passenger Compartment

"Compliments of the Highland Steamboat Company," Tony said, when he made another round of the passenger cabin armed with coloring books and crayons. Teddy and Ricky happily accepted theirs and set about coloring the tugboats, ferries, and whales, but Olivia was intent on eating the yellow crayon, which Helen gently pushed away from her mouth and back to the paper. Sean half-heartedly read some pages out of the book he had brought for the trip—a Zane Grey western—but mostly he basked in the glory of quality time with his family. He left his cell phone on the table, ready to take candid pictures of them. The cabin was quieter after the other passengers had all settled in for the crossing. Though they could more feel the vibrations than hear them, the giant diesel engines deep within the hull kept their steady beat. The boat's motion was not unpleasant, like the proverbial gentle rocking of the cradle of the deep.

The fog remained a blank canvas outside the windows.

The twins were so proud of their artistry that they soon showed their colorings to the young woman in the next booth. Which inevitably led to, "Hi, I'm Teddy. I'm Ricky. What's your name?" And Helen saying, "Boys, don't ask questions."

"Oh, they're adorable," the woman said. "I'm Abbey, and this is Ezra."

"Are you married?"

"Teddy," Helen said. "What did I just say?" Even though her own curiosity was piqued. There were no wedding bands on the couple who were so perfectly matched that they might be brother and sister, with fine features, beautiful clear skin, and gently curling hair.

"Actually, the wedding is in two weeks. We're on our *earlymoon*."

"I've heard of that," Helen said, delighted to meet a young couple embarking on the newest trend in weddings. They were calm, articulate, and soft-spoken, and Helen loved them immediately. Sean had noticed the small gold Star of David on a gold chain around Abbey's neck, so he said, "*Mazel tov*," with a nod to Ezra.

"Actually, it's Doctor Ezra," Abbey said. "He graduated from Harvard Medical School last week. He has to start his residency cycle at Massachusetts General Hospital right away, so there's no time for a traditional honeymoon. We'll do ours early, before the wedding."

"Abbey has another year of law school to go," Ezra said. He seemed slightly embarrassed at being introduced as a doctor, as if the reality were taking time to sink in. "Between us we have some big student loans to pay off."

"Not so big that he couldn't leave his new car behind," Abbey said. "If we'd flown to Nantucket, we'd already be in the honeymoon suite at the Jared Coffin House."

"We'll be able to drive around and see the island with the Lexus," Ezra said.

To which Sean said, "You'll never get out of that honeymoon suite, chum."

Helen wanted to hear all about the wedding. She moved to the next booth with Olivia, who was way too young to be enthused by romance. The toddler fell asleep while looking at the heretofore unknown eyes of their new friends.

"Come on over," Sean said, motioning for Ezra to join him and the twins. "You might as well hang with the guys. Once they get jabbering about weddings, you will not be able to get a word in there. Where do you live?"

"Boston."

"Boo, boo," the twins said in unison. "Red Sox suck."

"Easy there, sports fans," Sean said. He turned to Ezra. "We live near Shea Stadium, in Queens. I'm a cop, and Helen is a teacher."

"Police work must be interesting," Ezra said.

"It's a front seat on the greatest show on earth," Sean said. "I never thought I'd do anything else, since my father was a cop. But my brother is in prison—so go figure."

"Gee, I'm sorry about your brother."

"He belongs in there," Sean said. "It's a long story."

"So," Ezra looked at the twins. "Will you men join the police department?"

Ricky and Teddy loved being called men even more than they liked the suggestion of a career. But Sean said, "Well, my grandfather was also a cop walking a beat in the city, in the bad old days. I'm not sure the NYPD could survive a fourth generation of our family—especially being double-teamed by these rascals." He looked squarely into Ezra's eyes when he said, "I don't particularly care what they do for work, though. I just want them to be good men."

The boys stuck out their tongues and rolled their eyes, as if they had heard this bromide from their father all too often. Sean held his gaze on Ezra. Smiling slightly, he said, "Doctor, how do you feel about being married? The fun is over, you know."

"Yup. It is a big move, but I think I'm going to like it. How long have you been married?"

"About a dozen years, I guess. Helen could answer that better than me." He chuckled and said, "She keeps pretty close track of the months, days, and hours, you know."

"Ha!" Ezra said. "I get that. Sometimes I think Abbey has been counting the minutes since we met as undergraduates. Tell the truth, I know it was at a party—but I am not sure which party. We had classes together, and she was just sort of there one day."

"I heard that," Abbey said, across the booths.

"See, we're supposed to be honest with each other," Ezra said, with a twinkle in his eye. "Until we are. That's when we get into trouble."

"Honesty is highly overrated," Sean said. "It's not like I can come home from work with all the gritty details." Like wrestling a gun out of a perp's hand, went unsaid. "Sometimes we're better off holding our tongues—until the time is right."

"Always 'fess up!" Teddy said.

To which Ricky added, "Momma says it's always better to tell the truth."

Something about the boat is changing, Sean thought. He looked at the old Omega Seamaster on his wrist. The old mechanical timepiece had to be wound daily, but it had been his father's and it bore the patina of a man's life. Little paint spatters from maintaining a home and a boat. A faded leather band from years in fair weather and foul. Nicks in the crystal from some long-forgotten sidewalk skirmish with evil. Sean wore the watch the way some people used to wear POW bracelets— as a keepsake of his father—and a reminder that a man's time is finite.

It was too early to turn into Nantucket Harbor. Yet the boat's gait had changed slightly. He looked at his phone and saw that he had no cellular service. Not a glimmer of a bar was indicated. Few of the other passengers shared his concern. Except for the five men across the cabin. They had their cell phones out as well. Their heads were turning and leaning together, apparently whispering. One of them—with "14" on his shoulder—stood up and approached the crewmember making rounds of the passenger spaces. Mister 14 held his head too high, with his bearded chin out. Like a top-billed actor taking the stage. Like he was in charge of everything.

"Oh, one other thing," Sean said to Ezra. He discreetly touched the screen of his phone to bring up Google Maps. "After the wedding, get as far away from your parents as you can—both of your parents—until you need babysitters." The GPS on his phone did not rely on the cellular network and it showed that the boat had turned around, back toward Hyannis. "The grandparents only screw things up while you're getting to know each other. Let them spoil your kids, not your happiness."

The Engine Room

Bo was standing in the doorway to the engine room, which opened into an alcove on the freight deck, with an updraft of hot air and the cacophony of two diesel locomotive engines rising in the narrow steel stairway behind him. He watched as Grant and Todd spoke on the stern, and after Grant went up the stairway to the passenger deck, he waited for Todd to complete a round of the freight deck. He had the front of his coveralls unbuttoned to his waist and he backed into the shadows of the alcove when the young crewman came around toward the stern again, counting the steel frames that held the shape of the vessel's hull plating.

"Sprout, what are you doing?" Bo said, speaking from the half shadows of the alcove.

"Oh, hi, Chief," Todd said, when he turned to face the chief engineer. "I'm getting to know the ship. Why are you calling me Sprout?"

"That's what you are—a little sea-sprout—maybe you'll grow to be a real sailor someday. What makes you want to work here anyway?"

"I guess I just like boats."

"Uh-oh," Bo said, shaking his head. "Why do you like boats so much?"

"I don't know," Todd said. "I used to ride my bike over to the Cape Cod Canal, where you can get really close to the ships and tugboats when they come through. I like the way they move through the water and turn slowly in the current—the way the tugs pull giant barges with the roar of big diesel engines and then the big container ships come gliding past with a little plume of steam coming from the stack so quietly that you can hear the water rippling at the bow and the crew talking on deck."

"Oh boy," Bo said. "You've got it."

"What have I got?"

"Did you ever go to down to the shore and just look out to the ocean and wonder what is out there?" Bo said. "Did you ever wonder about the far shore?"

"Well, sure," Todd said. "Doesn't everybody?"

"Oh, you got it bad, Sprout—a real bad case of it."

"A real bad case of what?"

"It's one of the oldest afflictions of mankind," Bo said. "Boys have been standing on the coast looking at boats for centuries, yearning to go out on the ocean. They call it sea fever, and you've got a real bad case of it, I'd say."

"Gee, I never thought of it as an affliction."

"Oh, sea fever is a real sickness," Bo said. "The lucky ones get cured on their first voyage when they cry for home and get so seasick, they puke their guts out. But some poor souls cannot help themselves and they keep shipping out, even when they're cold and wet and tired from working all day and standing watch half the night. Those poor souls keep shipping out, year after year."

"Really, Chief?" Todd said. "They say that you've sailed every kind of ship in every ocean. Isn't it boring to just go back and forth from Cape Cod to Nantucket all day? I mean, where's the challenge?"

"The engines don't know where they're taking a boat, Sprout. An ocean, or a lake, or a river, it just don't matter to the engines. They just keep turning the big wheels. And I get to shut them down every night and go home. You'll see the glory of nights in your own bed eventually, if you ship out in blue water for a spell."

"But didn't you see great things on the deep sea?" Todd said. "Things you'd never see if you stayed home—typhoons and giant waves, tropical islands, and real pirates?"

"Ha!" Bo issued a hearty laugh. "That romance-of the-seas bullshit is for weekend blow-boaters and armchair sailors," he said. "Sure, I've seen all that and more, waves bigger than houses and grass huts alongside tropical lagoons with curving sandy beaches and palm trees like a postcard from paradise. Ha! I have also seen pitiful, starving wretches far from land on makeshift rafts trying to get away from the horrible place where they had the misfortune to emerge from their mothers' wombs. But most days at sea nothing happens—nothing at all—because mostly there is a whole lot of nothing between here and there. Oh, sure, a ship looks all important cutting through the waves with her flags flying and her big wheels churning the water—but after she passes—the ocean closes back up and settles down and Old King Neptune don't really give a shit if that ship was ever there or not. He also don't give a shit whether you sink or swim—it just don't matter to Old Mister Neptune. Don't you know the difference between being at sea and going to prison?"

"No, tell me."

"You can't drown in prison."

"Golly, Chief, why are you telling me all this bad stuff about ships?"

"No, don't get me wrong, Sprout. Seafaring is a fine life. You just need to go in the right direction."

"Which direction is that?"

"Down here," Bo said, pointing down the ladder into the depths of the hull. "You ought to work below the decks, unless you're afraid of hard, dirty, knuckle-busting work."

"The engine room?" Todd said.

"Now you're catching on," Bo said. "Trust me, Sprout. You would be better off forgetting about all that mate and captain stuff. The wheelhouse just aims the ship—the engine room makes it go. A smart boy like you should be a marine engineer." He handed Todd a pair of ear protectors. "Here, put these on. But first, do not call me Chief. My name is Bo Diddley."

"Bo Diddley?" Todd said. He clamped the ear protectors on his head and followed the chief down the steep ladder.

"That's right. Go look at my license hanging on the bulletin board," Bo said as they descended into the heat and infernal noise of the engineering spaces. "It says Bo Diddley Jacobs right on it, same as my birth certificate. Bo is a Scandinavian name if you didn't know." Bo took the steps one at a time, leading with his bum leg, the knee of which was reluctant to bend. "Now, a blue-blood Yankee boy like you probably don't know what Diddley means. I will tell you. That is Southern talk for scratch, or useless. 'That ain't worth diddley,' they say, down home. It is not an uncommon name on the Mississippi Delta, you know. It means I started from nothing, like the great guitar man Bo Diddley, who did his magic to turn the blues into rock 'n roll."

"Can I call you Bo?" Todd said. By then they were standing on the deck plates at the bottom of the ladder.

"Why else would I tell you?" Bo said. "Welcome to my kingdom."

Twelve feet below the car deck, they had descended into another world that was hidden from the passengers, not unlike the steampunk set of a post-apocalypse movie, where hot air was pulsed through by heavy machinery and minds were numbed by the infernal racket of diesel fuel exploding in the cylinders of two enormous railroad loco-motive engines. The deck plates in Bo's domain, which were bolted to a steel framework above the bilges, vibrated with the *largo* rhythm of the main propulsion engines and the *prestissimo* accompaniment of an entourage of auxiliary compressors, pumps, and motors.

"This here is Tina," Bo said, pointing to the closest engine. "That's Ike on the port side over there." These powerful twins were mounted close to the *Nighthawk's* keel and kept spotlessly clean under a sheen of oily residue, which made them glow in the overhead neon lights. "Ike gives me trouble now and then, like a fuel injection leak or a worn-out cylinder liner. But Tina here—Tina is a lady, and she just keeps the big wheels turning."

Bo put the white rag he used to wipe his brow into his back pocket and pulled out a red rag, which he used to wipe the railings and eve-rything else he touched in his kingdom. "These here are sixteen-cylinder units manufactured by the Electro-Motive Diesel division of General Motors," Bo said, yelling near Todd's ear to be heard close to the engines. "Each cylinder has a displacement of six hundred and forty-five cubic inches—that's over ten thousand cubic inches of dis-placement in each engine. Are you getting all this?"

"Sort of," Todd said. "What is that high-pitched whine, like a steam whistle?"

"These are the superchargers," Bo said, moving to the rear of the engines. "They're mechanical blowers to jam air into the cylinders. That's how we push four thousand horsepower out of each engine."

"Man, that's really dope," Todd said.

"Huh?" Bo said. "What do you mean, 'dope'?"

"Oh, dope is cool," Todd said. "You know, great."

"No, I don't know," Bo said. "Speak English, boy. Now, see this?" Bo led Todd to a watertight door behind the engines. "This here is shaft alley." He opened the door to reveal a long compartment where the shafts from each engine were rotating on pedestals with bearings. "That hydraulic ram all the way back there with all the pumps and gears controls the rudders." They went forward between Ike and Tina, with Bo pointing out the key features of each engine, and came to a large reinforced steel door at the front of the engine room. The door was wide open, but the powerful gears that engaged sawtooth racks to slide it open and shut made it obvious that this portal could be automatically closed at a moment's notice.

Inside the generator room, Todd was fascinated by the main electrical control panel, which he said was "classic" and "old-school." The panel stood in a cabinet in the middle of the room, ahead of the three generators, with a tall black façade that was made of non-conducting Bakelite phenolic resin. There was a wood handrail at waist height, and the face was festooned with banks of old-fashioned dials and control knobs the size of saucers. It all looked too large for the digital age, like a holdover from a black-and-white sci-fi movie.

"Now, you make sure you treat this door with respect," Bo said when they went through the opening again, back into the engine room. "It's important, because if the hull is filling up with water and the ocean gets into the engine room and the generator room at the same time, the boat is going to sink to the bottom, no doubt about it. Now, stand back!"

Bo twisted a black knob near the door and a loud bell jingled. For a few seconds nothing happened, but as the bell continued the gears turned and the door started to close. "This door will chop a piece of two-by-four lumber clean in half when it closes," Bo said. He picked up a smaller piece of lightweight dunnage lumber and held it in front of the door's knife-edge, which was steadily closing the gap. "You stand back now and watch what it does to this old scrap of wood."

"Wow," Todd said, eyes wide open when the door sliced the wood in half without slowing down as it sealed shut. "Man, this door is totally *lit*."

Bo managed to laugh at Todd's teen slang and reopened the door after his demonstration was complete. Then the old engineer sniffed at the air and said, "What's this?" He sensed a change in the boat's gait through the water. "Do you feel it?"

"Feel what?" Todd said.

"We're turning," Bo said. He moved to the small control console forward of the main engines, where a few truck-style gauges displayed the engines' revolutions, oil pressures, water jacket temperatures, and so forth. There was a waist-high desk with a big logbook, and above this was an electric gyro compass repeater indicating the ship's heading. "Look at that, Sprout—this old tub is turning all the way around, like we're going home."

The Forward Passenger Compartment

"Damien, are you okay?"

Grant said this when he was standing at the table near the snack bar where the youngest owner of the Highland Steamboat Company was lost amid a pile of printouts and reports.

"I'm fine," Damien said, raising his eyes to focus on Grant. "Why do you ask?"

"I was getting a little worried about you," Grant said. "You were staring off into space and didn't see me standing here. That's not like you."

"Oh, I'm sorry," Damien said as he pulled some of the papers closer and consolidated them into a single pile to make room across the table for Grant. "It's just these damn reports. Have a seat."

"Have you ever thought of investing in a briefcase?"

"I have a nice leather number I used at school," Damien said. He shoved the loose papers into the cover of his notebook. "But I can't bring it to work."

"I guess I knew that," Grant said with a smile. The family had built their business standing on mounds of sandblasting grit in the largest dry dock on Cape Cod, where each generation had to work at painting, welding, and sweating in the machine shop to keep their fleet of vessels operating. The children learned at an early age that any display of wealth or privilege was strictly *verboten*.

"It's okay. You know how my father is—he would abuse me to no end if I looked like a young executive. We must drive old pickup trucks to the office and do dirty work in the shipyard every day. When we get called in to deal with bankers, insurance guys, and lawyers, we have to sit in the office with grease and paint on our clothes."

"Your family works hard," Grant said. "Most people respect that."

"I guess," Damien said with a shrug. The ferry service had lower ridership in winter months, which was when the shipyard reached the peak of activity in the dry dock, so the owners had a full slate of work throughout the year. Almost all the profits went back into the ledger to fund repairs, new boats, and expanded service. "There has to be room for you to grow," his father would say, to justify why Damien's older brothers commanded much higher salaries than his youngest son. Although Roland distributed sizeable bonuses—if there was a profitable year—equally among the family. "How about you?" Damien said. "Is your sailboat in the water yet?"

"It's in," Grant said. "I'm thinking of selling it and getting a bigger boat, something we can use for some long trips."

Damien sat bolt upright when he said, "I don't like the sound of that, Grant."

"I have to retire sooner or later," Grant said. "I'd like sooner— maybe in two or three years."

"That's a relief," Damien said with a wry smile. "When you said long trips, I feared you already had one foot out the door." He looked around the passenger cabin before his eyes came back to Grant. "I remember that years ago, when I was a young kid, my father used to bring me down to this boat when you were in the shipyard doing maintenance. You would hand me a paintbrush and tell me to 'get to work.'"

"I always enjoyed that," Grant said. "Except that you got more paint on yourself than on the boat."

"You made work fun," Damien said. "You've always been that way."

"Well, before the boats I was a ski instructor—then I'd teach windsurfing and tennis in the summer—so work has always been like playing, I guess. I'll tell you something funny, though—some people get a ski instructor when they're really looking for a friend to talk to."

"You've always been good for that, too," Damien said. With a paintbrush in his hand, it had been easy to ask Grant those cryptic questions that preteens use to sort out their adolescent crises. Grant's most valuable insight was that he always gave clear answers to these murky inquiries. And he laughed at the right times.

"So?" Grant said, looking to where Katarina was working behind the food service counter. "Talk to me."

Damien paused while he too looked to where Katarina was serving customers, before he said, "It's complicated, Grant. I'm not sure— well—it's a mess, actually."

"It couldn't be that bad."

"It is," Damien said. "I like her—but that's the third rail with my dad. He cannot stand the thought of an employee marrying into the company. 'The pie can only be divided so many ways,' he says. He will be damned if a gold digger is going to get a penny. Especially an employee who is in the country on a work visa."

Grant said, "Have her quit and get some other job until he forgets she ever worked here."

"Katarina is here on a visa that the company arranged," Damien said. "The day after she doesn't work for us is the day she has to go home to Romania."

"Now I see the problem," Grant said.

"The thing is, I really like her. But if I show it, I could lose everything. Dad would take my share of the company away in a red second."

"That doesn't sound right," Grant said. "How can he take it away?"

"This whole thing is in a trust," Damien said. "Every year that we work we gain equity in the company, which has nothing to do with an inheritance. If I get fired—or quit—I cease getting equity."

"Uh-huh," Grant said.

"The thing is, I really, really like her." He paused and looked at Grant. He could not say this to anyone else in the company. He did not know why he was saying it to Grant. "You don't even know how great Katarina is. She is too damn modest. Did you know that she has a degree in mathematics?"

"Who knew?" Grant said. "But I did notice she has a really good head for numbers. She's amazing at spotting mistakes in the cash register tally."

"She's so sharp it scares me," Damien said. "We were driving up to New Hampshire one weekend—this is all just between me and you, of course—when she took this paperwork off the backseat of my car and started analyzing the numbers. She had it all figured out by the time we got off the thruway, and she gave me great ideas for ridership and expenses and the specials we could run. I should not be telling you this Grant—she is that smart. And I adore her."

"I hear you," Grant said. He looked away from Damien when something else grabbed his attention. "Do you feel that? I think we're turning."

"I'll tell you another thing," Damien said. Grant's question about the boat turning had not registered with him right away. "Sometimes I really want to walk away from the company. With two brothers ahead of me I will never be the boss, and Highland Steamboat only succeeds when one person has total control. One person must call all the shots, like my father. I know I could start my own business. It would not be easy. I'd have a lot to lose, but—"

"Damien, the boat is making a big turn."

"What? Maybe Tom is maneuvering around some lobster pots or sailboats."

"I don't think that's it," Grant said. There was nothing but gray mist outside the windows, and none of the passengers seemed aware of the course change. When he took a cigarette from his shirt pocket and placed it on the table both men watched it roll away. "We're heeling slightly to starboard," Grant said. "This feels like a really wide turn."

Katarina came out of the kitchen a moment later. "The captain is calling," she said, nodding at Grant. Before he stood up, Grant gave Damien a look that said, *something is up*. Tom would not call unless there was a problem.

Grant was on the growler phone in the kitchen for less than a minute before he motioned for Damien to join him. He was shaking his head in disbelief when he said, "Nantucket Harbor is closed. I never heard of such a thing, but they're not letting any boats in or out."

"That can't be right," Damien said. "There must be some mistake."

"It's a tough one to swallow, but Tom took the radio call himself. The Coast Guard told him flat out that the port was closed for several hours."

"For what reason?"

"That's the thing that bothers me," Grant said. "They wouldn't give a reason. Could it have something to do with the conference?"

"That's a safe bet," Damien said. "The Coast Guard is still going to have some explaining to do if they won't let a boat with a few hundred paying customers tie up to off-load."

Katarina was standing nearby, working in the kitchen with her back to the men. "Isn't your first lady visiting the conference today?" she said, without turning around.

"This doesn't look like the best day to pay a social call to the Nantucket Yacht Club," Grant said.

"Except that there are a few dozen billionaires at the yacht club this week," Damien said. "Every one of them a potential campaign donor."

"Do you think they'd close the island down for the first lady?" Grant said.

"I doubt that," Damien said. "I know for sure that the Feds didn't inform the company of any creditable threats. My father would have shut down all the boats today if we had that sort of warning, it would not be worth making the runs. What is Tom going to do?"

"Dana is on the helm," Grant said. "He's ordering her to make a very gradual one-eighty. In this pea-soup fog the passengers will not even notice that we have turned back, until we figure out what we are going to do."

"A U-turn?" Katarina said. "We're going back to Hyannis?"

"Unless you have a better idea," Grant said.

Katarina said, "Why not just stop and drift for a while?"

"Not for three hours," Damien said. "People panic when the engines stop on the crossing, even for one minute. We get more complaints about that than anything else."

"That's right," Grant said. "People are already on edge about seeing a wall of fog and mist outside the window. Nobody wants to get stuck on a boat in the middle of Nantucket Sound."

"If the captain made an announcement—" Katarina said.

"Half the passengers don't believe anything that comes over the public address speakers," Damien said. "We live in the age of distrust of authority. Some people jump past logic and go straight for conspiracy theories, so there would be plenty of drama if the boat stopped moving."

"Yup," Grant said. "We'll get everyone to the island eventually, but the office will have to come up with a new schedule for all the boats. Tom will let everybody know what's going on as soon as we have some facts."

"That works for me," Damien said. Then he turned to Katarina and said, "You'd better get ready for a rush of customers. It will be one free beer per customer on the way back to Hyannis."

"Of course," Katarina said. "In that case there should be free ice cream for the children, too."

"Good idea," Damien said. "The kids can have all the free ice cream they can eat."

They watched Katarina leave the kitchen. Her fluid movements added a bit of grace to an increasingly uncomfortable moment. Finally, it was Grant who said, "I hate to sound like one of your conspiracy nuts, Damien. I do not think the Coast Guard is telling us everything. If they went to the extreme of closing the port without telling us why, then something really big—really bad—must be in the wind."

5

FLASHPOINT

The Promenade

Tony was making his rounds of the passenger cabin when he noticed the turn. Some of the more seasoned passengers also sensed
the slight variations in the vibration of the propellers and the
change of the boat's gait through the water, and they stared out the
windows, vainly attempting to see something—anything—in the fog.
Their whispered doubts became a murmur of concern under the genial
conversations in the cabin.

A truck driver who was on the boat daily to make deliveries to the
island said, "What's up, Tony?"

"Hell if I know," Tony said. "We must be turning to avoid a sailboat,
or something."

"Sure," the trucker said. "Damn sailboats in the fog, right?"

Tony took a deep breath when he saw one of the working men sitting near the television rise from his seat and head across the cabin in
his direction. He knew he was about to deal with an unhappy customer
by the set of the man's jaw under his dark beard. Then too, there was
something unnatural about the way he walked in long strides, with his
arms not swinging.

The man didn't speak until he was up in Tony's face, where he said,
"Why are we turning around?"

"It's probably nothing," Tony said. He wanted to say, "relax, take it easy" to the man, who was seething with rage. But he knew better. "The captain might be helping a little boat that doesn't have radar. I'm sure he'll turn back toward Nantucket in a few seconds."

"That's not what this says," the man said, pointing to the map app on the screen of his smartphone. He was wearing some sort of foreign military field jacket with "14" embroidered on the shoulder. "This says we're headed straight back to Hyannis."

"I doubt we're going all the way to Hyannis," Tony said. "Anyway, the captain will make an announcement soon if there's a problem. Relax, he knows his business."

"Bullshit," the man said. "We need to arrive in Nantucket when you said we would. Timing is critical!"

"Take it easy," Tony said. "We don't even know how long the delay will be. We'll get you to Nantucket as soon as we can."

"You idiot!" the man said. "You're going to screw up this whole operation!"

"I don't know what operation you're talking about," Tony said. "Getting mad isn't helping. Please go back to your seat, and I will go find out what the problem is. Okay?"

"Idiot!" the man yelled. He pivoted around in a huff and moved toward the door to the promenade. "You're all idiots! You are dumb as a box of rocks! You're screwing with powers you can't comprehend!"

"Easy, man," Tony said. "We're all in the same boat."

Mister 14 stormed onto the promenade and turned toward the stairs leading to the freight deck. Tony followed and said, "Hey, you can't go down there now."

What Tony saw next made his heart sink.

Judd was standing on the promenade at the top of the stairs in a commanding pose—legs spread wide and hands on hips—blocking the man's path to the freight deck. Mister 14 rushed toward Judd with his fists clenched low at his sides. He was close enough that his angry spittle hit Judd's face when he said, "Get out of my way."

Judd was startled and took two steps back—almost falling down the stairs—before he reached into his vest and grabbed the butt of his gun. He was still pulling the long barrel of the .44 Magnum out of his shoulder holster when the man disarmed him with a practiced swipe across his chest—and then Judd was staring down the barrel of his own gun, thoroughly stunned when the stronger man shoved him aside.

"Are you deaf?" the man yelled. He stuck the muzzle of Judd's own gun under the security man's nose. "I said, get out of my way!"

Judd was terrified. Sweat drenched his brow. He farted and took several tentative steps to back away cautiously before he broke into an ambling, porcine run along the promenade deck, in full view of the passengers on the other side of the picture windows.

"Aw, shit," Tony said, as Mister 14 disappeared down the aft stairway to the car deck with Judd's gun. "This is going to be bad."

The Aft Passenger Compartment

Grant and Damien heard a commotion on the promenade before they saw Judd run past the window by their table, with snot dripping from his nose and teary-eyed panic on his face.

"Call the cops!" he said as he came into the forward compartment and rushed his bulk past the delicatessen, into the cocktail lounge, as far away from his assailant as possible. "Call the cops!"

"I saw it all," Katarina said, when she leaned over their table to speak in tones that would not be overheard. "Judd was trying to pull out his gun and a man took it away from him."

"What man?" Grant said. "Where is he now?"

"He looks like a soldier—in a green jacket with patches—and dark hair and a beard. He took Judd's gun and ran down the aft staircase to the freight deck."

"I'll alert the wheelhouse," Grant said. He called Tom on the growler phone behind the snack bar. Then he said, "Damien, we better check this out."

"Be careful," Katarina said, touching Damien's arm.

The two men walked aft through the forward compartment, where most people seemed unaware. But many passengers in the aft compartment had seen the confrontation on the promenade, so Grant and Damien were peppered with questions as soon as they entered, faster than they could answer.

"What's going on?" Or, "Is there a man with a gun on the boat?" And, "Are you going to do something?"

"Everybody, please remain calm," Grant said. "As a precaution, you can help by moving to the forward compartment in an orderly fashion while we figure this out. That's it—take your time—just leave your things and move all the way up there and find a seat. Thank you."

Damien noticed that the man he had seen with a badge at the snack bar—now with his family in tow—was leading the exodus to the forward cabin.

"Excuse me," Damien said. "Are you a police officer?"

"Not today," Sean said. "My family comes first."

"I understand that," Damien said. "We might need your help anyway."

"Wait until I get these kids to a safe place," Sean said. Then he held back and leaned into Grant and Damien when he said, "Listen, that phony soldier-boy was sitting with four other gentlemen, in front of the television. As soon as your security man did his little shit-and-run routine they all scattered—in different directions—like a practiced maneuver. You better take cover and call for heavy reinforcements."

The Ladies' Room

"Over here," Sean said. He pulled Helen aside in the passageway leading to the forward compartment and pushed open the steel door to the ladies' room, which opened inward to a sturdy privacy partition. The room was bright but austere, with neon lights in a hung ceiling. There were five toilet stalls, a row of sinks and mirrors, and two baby changing stations, but no windows.

"You kids get in here with your mother," Sean said.

Teddy said, "Dad, this is the girl's bathroom."

"It's okay," Helen said. "Get in here and play hide-and-seek with your sister under the sinks."

Sean stayed in the passageway long enough to urge some women with young children to follow Helen into the ladies' room, and a few did so. Others kept walking to the forward compartment, unable to make the snap judgment to believe a total stranger's advice to part with the migrating herd. In a crisis, who can you trust?

When he came back into the bathroom, Sean opened a small storage closet in the corner that was full of cleaning supplies. He handed the broom with the heaviest handle to Helen and offered others to the women, who declined to accept them. Except for one young black woman with dreadlocks and beads, who grasped a broom and understood the situation immediately. She said, "How many of them are there?"

"Five white males, at least," Sean said. Her eyes were clear and wide open, but they narrowed when he said, "They're the kind that won't like you very much."

There was no lock on the door, so he used his pocketknife to cut the lashings that were holding a large trashcan to the wall and tipped it over, spreading the contents just inside the entry door to trip an intruder. Some of the children were confused and started to cry.

"Leave this trashcan flat on the floor, lengthwise between the door and this partition," Sean said. "That will block the door. If someone tries to get in, use the broom handles to jab through the crack." He demonstrated by holding his hands as if to toss a javelin with two hands. "Jab, don't swing. Thrust with both hands and hit any intruder hard, in the face and where it hurts the most. Some of you can jab underhand, too."

"Stay with us," Helen said.

"I'll be right outside this door," Sean said.

Helen hugged him. "Be careful," she said. "I love you."

"Always," Sean said. He flicked off the lights in the bathroom and sidestepped out into the passageway. He paused for a few seconds until he heard the women slide the heavy trash can into place behind the door. He decided that when he came back here, he would take a position in the game room to guard the door. Then the aft passenger compartment was oddly empty, with abandoned personal articles strewn about, as he moved quickly toward the stairway to the freight deck.

6

FIRST BLOOD

The Freight Deck

Todd came out of the engine room and went across the freight deck to the stern, where the boat's wake disappeared into the fog. He had the handset for the growler phone in his hand and he was ready to spin the crank to call the wheelhouse to find out why the boat was turning when a bearded man in a tattered military jacket came down the stairs from the passenger deck.

"Sir, you're not supposed to be down here while the boat is under way," Todd said. "The captain will make an announcement when it is time to go to your car."

"Get out of my way, kid."

"But—" Todd said. He put down the phone and followed the man to a heavy-duty pickup truck with Michigan license plates, where the man unlocked the tailgate and the cap. When he began lifting heavy canvas bags, Todd said, "Hey, mister, you're not supposed to—"

He did not see the handgun in the man's hand until he raised it to bash the side of his head with the long barrel, which sent the young sailor reeling backward against another car and down to the deck.

Todd was motionless for what seemed like a long time. His eyes were open, but his eyelids were fluttering and he couldn't focus. He slowly became aware of his breathing and a strange chill sensation between his shoulders. He had landed on his stomach, with his cheek pressed against the gritty nonskid paint of the freight deck. The pulsing vibrations of the engines beneath the steel plates of the deck seemed to penetrate deep into his skull, where a colossal headache was overpowering his thoughts.

When his vision sharpened the world was sideways. There were men very close to him, but he could only see their feet and legs. They were hurriedly taking canvas bags from the pickup truck and putting on some sort of heavy vests. Their excited words sounded like indistinct buzzing in concert with the engines' vibration and the pain in his head.

One of the men, shorter and heavier than the others, stepped backward and tripped on Todd's leg, which made him drop something to the deck. "Damn it, be careful with that scope," another man said. The clumsy one cursed and turned to kick Todd, as if it were an unconscious person's fault that the rifle had been dropped.

The men stepped over and around him and left in different directions.

Todd's vision was fuzzy around the edges and his stance was shaky when he tried to stand up. He had been hit hard before—usually accidentally—in the inevitable collisions when boys play soccer and baseball and competitiveness overcomes caution. But he had never been in a real fight, beyond youthful tussles after middle school, and he thought that fights where boys' egos collided and bloody noses and split lips were inflicted were stupid. Yet he knew that this fight was different, that it was serious, and that everyone aboard the *Nighthawk* was in big trouble.

He stood with his legs spread wide, leaning on a car. He let go of the car one hand at a time, testing his balance. The one who had hit him and the other men were nowhere in sight, but when he saw another man come down the other stairs and walk quickly to a minivan on the very stern of the boat, he knew that he had to do something.

He leaned on cars when he moved with shaky steps toward the stern. He paused at a storage locker on the port side to take a dogging wrench—a ten-inch length of iron pipe—in his hand. Dogging pipes were kept near old-fashioned watertight doors to give more leverage when clamping the small levers, or dogs, to seal the door. But when he approached the man, who was pounding on the driver's side window of a family van and cursing, Todd had an entirely different use for the *dogger* in mind. He was determined not to lose another confrontation when he crept behind the man and raised the wrench with every intention of striking him on the head—hard—hard enough to really hurt a man.

Todd was taken by surprise once again when his new opponent spun around and grabbed the dogging wrench out of his hand. The man was lean and strong with short hair and a commanding voice, and he disarmed the young sailor with practiced ease.

"Perfect," the man said, examining the pipe he now held in his hands. "Where did you get this?"

"It's a dogging pipe for leverage on the handles to watertight doors," Todd said, half-falling, until the man caught him and held him up.

"Okay, stand back," the man said. He let go of Todd and tapped the side window of the van hard with the edge of the pipe, starting a shower of shattered safety glass as the window disintegrated. The van's headlights were flashing, and the anti-theft alarm was blaring. "I forgot that my wife has the keys in her bag," the man said. "Good thing you came along with this pipe."

"What are you doing?" Todd said.

"I need this," the man said, when he pulled a Glock pistol out from under the driver's seat. "Relax—I'm a cop. What happened to you? You're bleeding all over the place."

"A guy—he had a gun—he took some duffel bags out of his car—"

"A green military jacket and a beard?" Sean said. "Which way did he go?"

"I don't know—I was—down. There were some other guys. They all had guns. And I think they even had bulletproof vests, or something. Except one real big guy with a crazy beard—all he had was a big gun and coveralls, like a farmer."

"Okay," Sean said, lifting Todd's hand and guiding it to the gash above his ear. "You've got a nasty cut here. Hold direct pressure against it to stop the bleeding and get under one of these cars until this thing is over."

"I'm supposed to—"

"You've done enough," Sean said. "You've got balls, kid, but you can barely stand up."

Todd was not aware that Bo had come out of the engine room until the older man grabbed him from behind. "I got you, Sprout," Bo said, steadying the younger man. "Take it easy. You're coming back to the engine room with me."

"Take care of that kid," Sean said as he slipped the dogging pipe into his belt at the small of his back and readied his pistol for action. "Lucky for us that I saw his reflection on the window before he clobbered me. He's too damn brave for his own good."

The Cocktail Lounge

"Tony, what did you say to that guy?" Grant said after they had moved most of the passengers to the forward compartment and the cocktail lounge, the enclosed spaces closest to the bow.

"I was just trying to explain why we turned away from the island," Tony said. "So anyway, why did we turn around?"

"The Coast Guard closed Nantucket Harbor," Grant said.

"What? That is crazy. They can't do that."

"Yes, they can. The problem is that they won't tell us why the harbor is locked down."

"Look, we've got to find out what we're up against," Damien said. "We know that we have one man who is armed with Judd's gun. Is he a lone lunatic, or part of something bigger?"

"He was with four other guys," Tony said. "I don't see them now."

"I know who you're talking about," Grant said. "They've been aboard this boat a few times recently—five guys in a heavy-duty pickup truck with Michigan plates—they claim to be jobbers, working on the island."

"Then let's hope he's pissed off at those four other guys," Damien said. "This could be a workplace dispute for all we know—we might just be caught in the middle."

"The turnaround set him off," Grant said. "It's hard to believe that some guy would be that peeved about missing out on a job on the island. We'd better hope those guys were not planning to do something really bad on Nantucket today—that conference is a big target. We could have terrorists onboard for all we know."

"No way," Tony said. "They don't look like terrorists to me."

"Nobody knows what terrorists look like," Damien said. "Until they start killing people."

"Since Judd is useless, I'm going to have to go down to the freight deck myself," Grant said. "It will be better if we find this guy before he comes up here shooting."

"I'm going with you," Damien said.

"Count me in," Tony said.

"Tony, you and Katarina should stay with the passengers," Grant said. "When the off watch gets down here, keep them with the passengers, too. If this guy is a shooter, hide under tables if you must—just don't let anybody panic and jump overboard. With the cold water and the fog, we'll never get the jumpers back alive."

7

ALL HANDS ON DECK

The Promenade

The cribbage players were startled when Dana bust into the galley spreading the alarm. "There's trouble down below," she said. "Somebody has Judd's gun. Tommy wants us to lock all the doors up here so no one can get into the wheelhouse."

"Let's go," Lou said when they threw down their cards. "Saint and I will take the aft stairs. Dylan, you and Butch take the forward stairs."

"Right, but what do we do if this guy starts shooting?"

"Improvise," Lou said. "And keep your head down. When he turns his back—or runs out of ammo—we rush him."

"Wait, Justin," Dana said. "Tom wants me and you to lock up the galley and the crew's quarters and stay with him."

"Sweet Jesus," Justin said. "Can't I ever serve lunch on time? It's one gosh-darned thing after another on this boat."

The off watch left Justin and Dana inside and dashed out of the galley. They split up on the sundeck as Lou had suggested. Fog hung over the world outside like a gray shroud across the sky.

"Slow down," Lou said when Saint sprinted across the sundeck toward the aft stairs. "Don't run until we see the situation."

"Screw that," Saint said. "I'm going to tackle this bastard and ask questions later."

Saint and Lou were halfway down the stairs to the open promenade deck around the passenger cabin—which appeared to be completely deserted—when a bearded man in a camouflage hunting jacket stepped out from behind a ventilator and raised the ugly shape of an AK-47. The assault rifle barked three times and Saint tumbled heels over head down the stairs.

Lou was exposed on the stairs, with too much momentum to turn back. He instinctively got small and crouched to his left and leaped over Saint to get at his assailant, who continued to fire—these two shots went wide—then Lou was on the shooter, pushing the weapon aside, allowing hand-to-hand training from fifty years in the past take over. The entire world was blurry and flickered in Lou's mind for a moment like a cold neon light coming on, erasing the decades separating the old fisherman from the insanity of the battlefield, and in an instant he was back in combat. His open palm struck the other man's jaw hard and continued around his neck into a headlock-throw that sent the man down, until he landed with his back against the railing separating the promenade from the water. The other guy was taller and heavier than the old fisherman, but the bigger man was down and terrified and shouting stupid words—begging for help from his friends— he was calling for someone named Matthias—when Lou gritted his teeth and kicked him in the face as hard as he could until he shut up.

The old fisherman reached down and grabbed the dazed man by his collar and belt. He was heavier than a man should be—Lou realized then that the man had body armor under his jacket and bandoliers of ammunition over his shoulders—but Lou was devoid of feelings when he grunted and tossed the other man feet-first over the railing. It meant no more to him than shoveling trash fish over the side after emptying the nets back when he was fishing for a living. The man tried to hold on, and when he looked up Lou saw what his steel-toed work boots had done to the other man's face. He felt absolutely nothing as the man fell into the water with a splash. The *Nighthawk* was still moving through the water at full speed, so he disappeared quickly and went straight to the bottom.

Saint was a goner. His mortal remains were a bloody heap at the bottom of the stairs, but Lou felt nothing more for the man he had worked with, and eaten with, and laughed with for years than he felt for the man he had just killed—in combat there was only the living and the dead, and remorse for the fallen came later. Lou had tried to erase from his mind what a high-power assault rifle at close range can do to a human body, but when he saw Saint's broken corpse, he knew then that those haunting memories would never really leave him. When he reached to the deck and picked up the hated weapon where the other guy had dropped it—a Russian-made AK-47 with a pistol grip and an extended thirty-round magazine, probably at least twenty rounds remaining—he was back in Saigon, back in the brutal urban close combat around the embassy in the final days.

He had come home to Chatham and gone back to commercial fishing and drinking to excess. He got married and bought a house and raised a family—that was what you're supposed to do, wasn't it?—but the night terrors had not eased off until years after he quit the booze. He never talked about the war, and most people did not even know that he had been one of the ones to go.

It would have sickened the old fisherman to hold this hated chosen weapon of his enemy once again, if he had the luxury of time to think about it. The AK-47—also called the "Kalashnikov" or simply "AK"— was the standard weapon of the Russian and Soviet military since 1947 to the present day. Over one hundred million of these killing machines had been manufactured, with most of them aimed against democracy, freedom, and individual liberty. Lou was ambivalent about most firearms—they were just tools—but the sight of an AK-47 sickened him in ways that he could never explain to anyone who had not been on the receiving end of their firepower. He would prefer to toss this weapon over the side, except that his adversary had called out to several friends for help. There was more than one murderous accomplice onboard.

Lou walked into the passenger cabin with the AK-47 at the ready—not sure he wanted to live with the dreams again—yet he had a job to do.

The Lower Hold

Dylan and Butch came down the forward stairs and met a rush of passengers who had exited the passenger compartments and run toward the bow on the promenade when the gunshots were heard. When the panicked group reached the open area on the bow, they could see that most of their fellow travelers were on the other side of the windows, packed uncomfortably tight into the cocktail lounge.

Someone said, "There's no room inside for us!" Dozens of others said, "Where can we go?"— "Where are the life jackets?"— "I can't believe this is happening." Others still said, "They're shooting on the boat," as if everyone had not already heard gunshots.

One man in a Charles River Country Club windbreaker grabbed Dylan by his shirt and said, "I demand you call a Coast Guard helicopter to get me off this boat."

"That's not going to happen," Dylan said. "We're all leaving together. Follow me and I'll take you to a safe spot."

"Everybody, this way," Butch said, even though he was not yet sure where Dylan would lead the group. "Stay calm and follow that crewmember."

When Dylan opened the heavy door and started down the stairs to the freight deck, some passengers doubted his wisdom. "But—I saw the bad man run downstairs," one woman said.

"She's right," another man said. "The shooter went down to the cars. I saw it all."

"I don't doubt that," Dylan said. "But they are up on the passenger deck now, and the danger is at the other end of the boat. The freight deck is huge, and with all the cars and trucks they won't see us."

"Where are you taking us?" a woman said as they went down the enclosed stairway.

"To a very safe place," Dylan said. "Trust me."

At the bottom of the stairway, Dylan looked aft on the freight deck. "Okay," he said. "It looks good so far. Just wait here while I unlock the next door."

There were car alarms with flashing lights going near the stern, but he did not see anyone there. Dylan stayed low when he moved between the vehicles parked close together on the freight deck. He had grown up in an old Cape Cod family that still held to values of integrity and self-sufficiency. The family farm was not large, but it served as the hub of a modest empire that included boarding stables, a lumber mill, beehives, a produce stand, and a small boatyard on the Bass River, surrounded by a rising tide of upscale suburban homes. The family had always survived there by hard work and ingenuity, so Dylan was always thinking ahead. Which was why he went to a cubbyhole in the partition between the narrow alley where cars were parked and the center section full of trucks and large vehicles. He faced a heavy steel door inside the cubby, which was locked, and he felt around over the frame where the key was hidden.

"Damn it," he said, when his fingers could not locate the key. Then he said, "Son-of-a- bitch," when he fumbled the key and it fell to the deck with the ring of brass landing on steel.

He realized that his hands were shaking when he picked up the key and inserted it into the large industrial deadbolt lock above the doorknob. *God, let this be the right thing to do,* he thought. *I could get all these people killed if I'm wrong.*

When the door opened, he was standing above a narrow stairway that led to a storage hold that ran from side to side under the freight deck. There was an electrical panel on the bulkhead, and he reached in and started flicking circuit breakers. As he did so the neon lights far above on the ceiling of the enclosed freight deck went out, row by row, like the blocks of a city descending into a blackout. Since the bow vehicle loading doors were closed, when he snapped the last circuit breaker, the only light on the rows of parked cars and trucks was coming through the large stern opening. The forward section of the freight deck was then in darkness, and anyone approaching from the stern would be backlit and easy to spot.

Dylan went back to the stairway and said, "Follow me. It is dark, so hold on to each other. And stay calm."

In the alcove at the top of the stairway, Dylan took a man who looked capable and fit by the arm—it was the country club member who had demanded a helicopter. "This stairway is really steep and narrow," Dylan said. "You stand at the bottom and be ready to catch anybody who falls. Got it?"

"I'll do it," the man said, suddenly cooperative when he had a job to do. He went down first and stood ready as instructed.

Dylan counted the passengers as they went down the stairway. He had taken sixty-one lives on a gamble that he hoped would pay off. There was nothing else he could do on the freight deck. He locked the door from the inside and went down the stairs into the hold himself.

Butch had found a Navy-style battle lantern and he shined the beam on the faces of the passengers, who were looking at the crewmen and wondering what was next.

"I'll go up after a while and see what's going on," Dylan said. "In the meantime, we're safe here. Let us all be quiet and wait."

A young voice from the back of the group said, "I have to go the bathroom."

"There's a dark corner full of cleaning supplies behind you," Dylan said. "Do what you have to do. We're all in this together."

"Man, the lights," Butch said. "That was good thinking."

"Yup, we've been lucky so far," Dylan said. His satisfaction was in knowing that his father—if he were still alive—would bestow his ultimate compliment on seeking this haven for so many people. "Clever, son. Very clever," his father would have said. Then he took off his company shirt and put it back on, inside out, to hide the large block letters that said "CREW" across the back.

8

BLOOD LUST

The Cocktail Lounge

The *Nighthawk*'s cocktail lounge could normally accommodate fifty patrons in a space encircled by a plush settee under large windows on three sides, with tables and chairs in the center. But the situation after five distant gunshots were heard on the promenade was far from normal, and more than twice that number were huddled there, with their whispers and crying blending into a buzz that made the lounge sound like a giant beehive. A few dogs that had been separated from their masters ran excitedly around the passenger deck near the entrance to the lounge, finding each other and reverting to pack behavior.

Katarina was behind the bar, trying to hide the children. She sent some of the smaller ones behind the kegs of beer under the long counter by making a game of it, while others refused to leave their parents' arms. The door to the small utility closet behind the bar, which was only large enough to contain a mop bucket and brooms, was locked—which it had never been before. So she urged parents to allow their children to conceal themselves behind the bar and under tables, even though she could not be heard over the other voices—until the single gunshot that seemed to come from directly overhead was heard.

The closer shot elicited a collective gasp, punctuated by stifled screeching, which settled into deathly silence as people pushed mothers with babies and toddlers toward the concealment and comparative safety under the heavy bar. Others ducked and covered under the tables and even tried to hide between chairs.

One panicked man said, "We've got to get off this boat!"

The man bolted out of the lounge and made it to the doors to the promenade deck, nearly starting a stampede of terrified passengers, with Tony in hot pursuit. He was climbing over the railing to jump into the water rushing by thirty-six feet below—the boat was still moving through the fog at cruising speed—when Tony grabbed him.

"Don't be an idiot," Tony said. "You won't last fifteen minutes in that cold water."

Tony dragged the man back to the lounge and tried to reassure the group. "Let's all stay calm," he said. "The trouble is at the other end of the boat. We're safer if we stay together here."

"That's right," Katarina said, holding her head high to be heard by everyone in the lounge. She forced herself to remain serene, even though the single gunshot from above might have come from the wheelhouse. "We should remain calm and let the crew deal with the situation."

Someone said, "Where are the shooters now?"

"They could be anywhere on the boat," Katarina said. "But they're not here. Perhaps the crew will find them before they find us."

A young woman said, "How many of them are there?"

"I don't know," Katarina said.

"What will we do if they come in here?"

"Maybe we can reason with them," Katarina said. "If we all stay calm."

"But if they start shooting—?"

"Then we rush them." Tony said. "We pile on and wrestle them down. They can't shoot all of us."

The passengers hardly noticed that the *Nighthawk* had begun rolling from side to side. The motion was gentle at first, but each roll gained momentum, until it became undeniable as napkin holders slid off a side counter and glasses fell off tables. When bottles of alcohol rolled off the top shelf and crashed behind the bar with shattering glass and splattering booze, people reached for something solid—and each other—to keep from falling. Katarina said, "Tony, this isn't right. The water is calm, so why is the boat rolling side to side so hard?"

"Somebody who doesn't know how to drive a boat is spinning the helm," Tony said. With sea legs conditioned by decades on heaving decks, he alone stood easily and seemed nonplussed by the motion of the boat. "They're over-controlling like mad."

"Is it dangerous?"

"Not if everybody holds on tight," Tony said. The rolling became so severe that the chairs in the lounge began to slide across the deck. Then some people fell, and they too slid across the deck until other passengers held them.

"This wild ride could be part of some plan to frighten the passengers," Katarina said as she held onto the bar to keep from falling herself.

"It's working," a man standing nearby said, as he too grasped the bar. "Can't you stop this?"

"Everybody sit down on the deck," Tony said, loud enough to be heard in every corner. "The boat is designed to handle heavy seas, so it can't roll too far. We'll be okay."

"Let me off this boat," a man said, after one person became sick. When another person vomited, the stench set off a chain reaction.

"This is ridiculous," a woman said, when the tension and *mal de mar* became unbearable. "We can't go on like this!"

The growler phone in the kitchen squawked; Katarina went to it and heard Grant's voice. "We can't find anyone on the freight deck," he said. "And there is no answer in the wheelhouse. What is going on up there? Are you okay?"

"Yes," Katarina said. "Except for this terrible rolling motion. Did you hear those three gunshots from the promenade? And we just heard another gunshot from above—pray they are not into the wheelhouse. People are very afraid. But we are—" Katarina halted in mid-sentence when a woman in the lounge screamed. Then she said, "Grant, they are here! Outside the windows on the promenade."

A wave of panic surged across the lounge when three masked figures holding military-style assault rifles appeared on the promenade deck outside the lounge windows. The attackers looked like storm troopers, with boots and facemasks. The leader was a large man in an armored vest, who moved along the promenade with confident strides, followed by a man who was shorter and heavier, wearing identical armor. An exceptionally large man in bib coveralls brought up the rear. He alone wore no body armor or mask, as if his bulk alone made him bulletproof, and the scraggly gray beard that reached his belly was a mask in itself. They walked quickly along the promenade deck and entered the cabin at the door near the snack bar.

"Hey, no—n—no guns in here," Tony said, standing between the attackers and the passengers at the entrance to the cocktail lounge, with his stutter out of control. "Somebody could get hurt."

The leader gave no warning when he raised his rifle and fired into Tony's chest, sending the strongman reeling to the deck. The deafening report of the shot reverberated around the enclosed space and caused many of the passengers—who were now apparently hostages—to recoil and cover their ears. Then there were screams and stifled sobbing as the passengers cried in horror, which became a collective murmur of "Dear God, this can't be happening."

While the attackers glared at the passengers and waved their weapons menacingly, Katarina went to Tony's side. She knelt next to him and took his hand as his chest heaved with his final labored breaths, even while the leader stepped closer and showed his contempt for the dying man by kicking his body with the toe of his boot.

"Anybody else have any bright ideas?" the leader said as he pulled his mask down and stood over his kill with his chest puffed up, like a big game hunter in his moment of murderous glory. He had a prominent jaw under a close-cropped black beard and menacing gray eyes under a dark brow. The number "14" was embroidered on his shoulder.

"Yes," Katarina said, with surreal calm. She knew what had to be done, because she came from a part of the world where strongmen took what they wanted when the rule of law faltered. "Let the children move to a safe place. You don't want to harm them."

"Who are you?"

"I am Katarina, the food service manager on this boat," she said.

"Please don't harm any of these people. We won't give you any trouble."

"You're in the crew? What's with the accent?"

"I am from Romania."

He mocked the Slavic edge on her accent when he said, "Okay, Bride of Dracula, what's wrong with this damn boat? Why is this fricking piece of crap trying to roll itself over?"

"One of your group must be driving," Katarina said. So at least this miserable motion was not part of their plan. "The steering on this boat is extremely sensitive. Any crewmember would know not to over-control at high speed."

"That dumb-ass Zack," the leader said when he turned to his cohorts. "I knew he was lying when he said he knew how to drive a ship." Then he took a small radio out of a pocket on his body armor and spoke into it. "Zack, what the hell are you doing up there? Come back."

There was no answer from Zack, and Katarina tried not to let her expression reveal that she now knew that her tattooed former employee was one of the terrorists, with a key role in the attack. He was in the wheelhouse, trying to take the *Nighthawk*—and all the souls onboard—somewhere they did not wish to go.

"There's too much steel around us," the big man in the coveralls said. "Those cheap radios won't work inside the boat."

"Damn it, Behr," the leader said. He tossed the useless walkie-talkie aside. "Go up there and kick that fairy Zack in the ass. Tell him to get a grip. If he can't drive the damn boat, just put a bullet in his head and steer this piece of shit yourself."

"That would be a pleasure," Behr said as he turned to leave the lounge.

"Wait a minute," the leader said. "Give me your choker before you go."

"Okay," the big man called Behr said, as he pulled an ugly weapon out of a satchel at his waist. The sawed-off shotgun had two barrels that were only about ten inches long, with a stock that had also been chopped down to six inches behind the triggers. As he handed the weapon to the leader, he looked at Katarina when he said, "I still get to use this later, right?"

"Yeah, sure," the leader said as Behr left the lounge. Katarina nearly fainted when she saw that a loop of wire had been bolted to the cut-off shotgun's muzzle, but she quickly overcame the wave of fear that nearly overpowered her.

"It would also be helpful if he slowed the engines down," Katarina said. "Where is he taking us at full speed?"

"We're going to Nantucket," the leader said. "I'm not calling this mission off."

"What is your name?" Katarina said, hoping to reason with the leader. "What is it that you want?"

"You, of all people, ask what we want?" he said. "We want to restore higher moral values in this land. It's disgusting how women like you dress and act—look at yourself!—you are a temptress! The Bible tells us that 'Charm is deceitful, and beauty is in vain.'"

"Yes, I know that passage," Katarina said. "It is from Proverbs, and the rest of it says, 'but a woman who fears the Lord is to be praised.'"

"New rules, bitch," Mister 14 said, with a rising edge of anger in his tone. He let his assault rifle hang from a strap around his neck and held the shotgun by the grip behind the trigger guard with his left hand and easily passed the wire loop over Katarina's head, twisting the gun several times to tighten the noose. "From now on, you speak when spoken to. Got it?"

She kept her hands at her side and nodded *yes*, while looking squarely into his eyes, breathing deeply and slowly to relax the features of her face so as not to betray the fear and anxiety that lay beneath. She knew that the smell of blood and death was in the air and that she would have to use every tool she had at her disposal to survive. Every carefully chosen word, every expression, and even the slight movement of her eyes mattered. She knew that he was the leader, that he was left-handed, his eyes were pale gray like a wolf's, that he knew no shame, and that his finger was on the trigger of a shotgun fastened to her neck.

She also knew that God was watching, and for the second time in her life she prayed for Him to grant her the strength to find a way to see another day.

9

THE DEAD ZONE

The Game Room

The *Nighthawk* was speeding through the fog and rolling side to side like a logging truck with no brakes careening down a mountain road when Sean came up from the freight deck on the starboard side. His pistol was in his hand and the pipe he had taken from Todd was tucked into the small of his back. He had heard the first three shots followed by two shots from the port-side promenade, and then the single shot from above—he guessed it was the wheelhouse—and finally another single shot from the cocktail lounge. It seemed that the shooters were sweeping though the boat searching for targets. So he stayed low on the promenade and crouched under the big windows to look into the aft passenger cabin, which appeared to be deserted. He knew that he would have to go inside to find a secure position from which he could cover the door to the ladies' room. The video game room was still his first choice, so he entered the cabin cautiously—and came face-to-face with a wiry old man wearing a black wool hat and hefting an AK-47.

Sean held his fire and sidestepped to cover behind a support column. This guy looked more like a hardworking sailor than a terrorist. But where did he get an AK?

"Who the hell are you?" the man said.

"I'm on the job," Sean said, staying in cover and instinctively offering the phrase he would use to identify himself to another cop in the city. Then he remembered that he was far from the streets of Manhattan, and he said, "I'm a cop. Who are you?"

"I'm in the crew," Lou said, lowering the muzzle of his weapon. "Damn, I'm glad I didn't shoot first."

"So am I," Sean said, coming out from behind the bulkhead. "Be careful where you point that cannon, my friend."

"No problem," Lou said. "You don't look like one of them. I took this Kalashnikov from a filthy bearded prick wearing tactical gear. And I'm pretty sure he was not alone."

"I know exactly who you're talking about," Sean said. "Let's take cover. We better see them before they see us."

"Right," Lou said as he followed Sean to the game room. One of the double fire doors was propped partially open by a stray trash can, allowing some visibility to the forward passenger compartment. Lou shut off the overhead lights in the game room once they were inside. When they were out of sight, Sean said, "Where did you learn how to fight?"

"In rice paddies full of shit," Lou said. "At the end, I was in Saigon."

"That's the first good news I've had today," Sean said, nodding to Lou. Having a veteran of urban combat armed with an AK on his team was as good—maybe better—than having another cop as backup.

Grant and Damien passed Saint's body when they came into the cabin from the port side, both men looking visibly bewildered and upset by what they had seen. Lou waved them into the game room, where Grant said, "Oh my God, is that Saint?"

"It's him," Lou said. "I was on the stairs right behind him when he bought it."

"Where is the guy who shot him?" Damien said. "And how did you get that weapon?"

"That guy fell overboard."

There was a stunned moment before Grant said, "Lou, what did you do?"

"The guy who finished Saint got what he deserved," Lou said. He spoke with no more emotion than if he was grousing about an empty coffeepot in the galley. "His own body armor and spare ammo took him down." Lou held up the assault rifle for the others to see. "He dropped this before he went over the side, and straight to the bottom."

"I can't believe it," Grant said. "Saint was sitting down to play cards in the galley—"

"We don't have time for that," Sean said. "Who's in charge here?"

The crewmen and the cop all looked at each other for what seemed like a long moment in which nothing was said. Finally, Damien said, "Sorry, Grant, we have to assume the worst about Tom Chapman. You're the captain now."

"Okay," Sean said. "Now that we have that settled." He turned to Damien and said, "You are not in a crew uniform, so who are you?"

"My family owns these boats."

"Doesn't that make you top dog?" Sean said.

"No. Grant has the license and he was signed on as mate. That makes his word law."

"Fine," Sean said. "Then listen to me, Grant. There are shooters with assault weapons and body armor on this boat. We need a SWAT team with heavy weapons and combat medics, pronto. Did someone transmit a radio distress call?"

"I can't be sure," Grant said. The cop's question about who was in charge had caught him off balance. Damien was right. That gunshot from above, and the zigzag wake that the boat was now trailing meant—although it was impossible to believe—that Tom was probably one of the first casualties.

"Our cell phones aren't going to help," Damien said. "We're in the middle of Nantucket Sound—the cell tower dead zone."

"What do you suppose they're doing with the passengers?" Grant said, looking directly at Sean. "I was on the growler with Katarina when the shooters came into the cocktail lounge. Maybe keeping those people together was a mistake."

"You did the right thing sending everyone to one place," Damien said. "People jumping overboard is the nightmare scenario. We'd never get back to them in time."

"That's right," Lou said. "This time of year—fifteen, maybe twenty minutes in the water—it would all be over. We had to keep them inside."

"Don't second-guess yourself," Sean said. "Think about the next decision. We must let the Coast Guard know how bad our situation is. We need help now, and a few lightly armed kids in a little boat with a pretty flag and a blue light on the roof are only going to get themselves killed. We need a full response from the FBI and the state police. They better be getting aboard helicopters already."

"The only radios are in the wheelhouse," Grant said. He had made his decision. He knew what had to be done first, and he knew that he was the one who had to do it. "If we're lucky, there is only one bad guy in there. Maybe we can do something about him and retake control of the boat. But I'll need some help to get into the wheelhouse."

"Me and you," Lou said to Grant. "I'll go up to the sundeck ahead of you, but you've got to understand the rules." Lou looked to Sean, who nodded affirmatively, knowing what the old warrior was about to say. "It's us or them. We need to move under cover and kill those guys before they even know we're there."

"Got it," Grant said as the reality of their situation became clear—the bad guys weren't going to give them any warning shots, either. He had played enough paintball with his sons in the forests near their home to know that even the best players get splattered eventually. But this was no game. "Do what you have to do, Lou. Just get us to a radio."

The Engine Room

"Sprout, you are really a sight now," Bo said as he opened the first aid kid and wrapped a gauze bandage around Todd's head. The young sailor was sitting on a tool chest in a corner of the engine room with blood on his shirt and a dizzying headache. "How are you feeling now?"

"I'm going to be sick, Bo," Todd said. The boat was rolling from side to side so hard that a small pump that Bo had been overhauling slid off the workbench and crashed to the steel deck plates alongside the starboard engine, followed by a shower of wrenches and screwdrivers. "I need to get out of this engine room," Todd said. "I can't stand the noise, and the smell of hot oil is getting to me."

"You sit right there, Sprout," Bo said. "It isn't safe topside right now, and you're in no shape to defend yourself, much less help. You best stay down here with me."

"What the hell is going on, Bo?"

"Heck if I know. Far as I can tell this started with some yahoo running around the boat with a gun, and that policeman you almost brained with a dogging pipe was chasing him. That's bad enough, but you say you saw more men with guns on the freight deck. Are you sure about that? Because what really bothers me is that this boat is rolling like a pig in mud on a hot day, and Captain Tom isn't picking up the growler phone in the wheelhouse—and that never happens."

"Bo, we've got to see what's going on topside."

"Hang on, Sprout," Bo said. "Let's not rush into anything."

"Bo, I'm supposed to be on watch on the freight deck. I've got to go up there."

"Listen, Sprout, that door to the freight deck is blocked from the inside with a crowbar, and I'm not going to open it right now—because this is my kingdom, Sprout. If the bad guys get in here, they have total control of the boat. They can do whatever they want with this boat and everyone on it once they get in here, and we can't let that happen. Besides, I need your help right here."

"What can I do?"

"Can you steer a boat by a compass?" Bo said.

"Of course, I can," Todd said. "That's easy. But how can I steer the boat down here?"

"Sprout, don't they teach you anything at that maritime kindergarten? Come here to the main control panel. See, there is a gyrocompass repeater above the panel. Now look, this lever is a shuttle valve that controls the steering motor. All I do is push this knob, and—there we go—now we have control of the steering down here. What's the heading back to Hyannis?"

"Well, I think Captain Tom usually tells me to steer three hundred and fifty degrees by the big magnetic compass in front of the helm. But the gyrocompass indicates true north, right? We'd have to subtract fourteen degrees for the westerly variation around Cape Cod. I guess I should steer three hundred and thirty-six degrees per the gyrocompass."

"Well, good," Bo said. "Maybe they do teach you something in school. Now, go ahead and steer."

"No, there's more, Bo." Todd produced the *Eldridge's* book from his back pocket and turned to the tide tables for Nantucket Sound. "What time is it? I think the tide is ebbing, right? We better steer a few degrees farther west. I'd hate to hit those rocks at Bishop and Clerks Reef."

"Damn, boy," Bo said. "You are a smart little sprout. You figured that out just like a real master mariner."

"I don't know about that," Todd said. The violent rolling stopped as he steadied the boat on course with the little lever that served as a standby tiller. "Except how do we know that Captain Tom wants to go back to Hyannis? We were halfway across, so why not steer for Nantucket?"

"You just keep the boat steady, Sprout. You're doing fine." Bo took the handset for the growler phone in his hand and twisted the dial to select the station to call. "There's no answer in the wheelhouse but let us see if Justin is awake in the galley. Deckhands are full of scuttlebutt, but the cooks on a ship always have the straight scoop. You best remember that, Sprout."

The Galley

Justin looked out to the empty benches and the rows of life raft canisters on the sundeck through a small square window in the heavy steel door in the galley. The large mirrored glass window over his prep area would have offered a broader view, but the reflective coating there was not perfect, and sometimes those outside could see dim images of the interior. Since he and Dana had caught occasional glimpses of a gunman roaming the sundeck, the smaller window behind a heavy steel door seemed a better option.

"What's going on out there?" Dana said. She was standing next to him, breathing hard. Her heaving chest had not calmed since they had first heard footsteps on the overhead, and the sudden gunshot from the wheelhouse. Since then, Tom was not answering the growler phone. And he was certainly no longer in command of the *Nighthawk*, which was rocking and rolling as if a troupe of dancing monkeys had taken the helm.

"Nothing," Justin said. In happier times his view of the sundeck from his galley was not bad. The best scenery came on sunny days, when women would stretch out on the benches in front of his one-way window to sunbathe. They had to know that someone would be watching from behind the mirrored glass, which might be why the gals with the best bodies often got closest to his vantage and flirted with modesty. Which was fine. Although he hated it when children would tap on the glass and ask if anybody was in there. Justin did not much care for children, anyway. He much preferred dogs—he liked dogs better than most people, and he would always take out a bowl of water out to an animal lying on the hot deck, especially if he might pass close to a sun goddess. "Not a darn thing but fog out there right now," Justin said.

"You're sure the door is locked?" Dana said. She bumped against him when the boat took a heavy roll.

"Hell yes, it's locked," Justin said. "He already tried to get in here once, remember?"

"I know," Dana said. They had heard a gunman on the other side of the door more than once since the nightmare began. "Sorry, I'm just a little scared out of my wits."

"You and me both," Justin said. He smiled at her, for once not caring that the gap where he was missing an incisor tooth was showing. After twenty-three years on the boats, he no longer regretted that he had not become a nut farmer, which had been his original plan. Until he lost the prime land and nearly two hundred immature pecan trees in the divorce. The good thing about that dashed dream was that he could often say, "I used to be a nut farmer, now I work with the nuts on these boats."

"I have a feeling me and you are going to come out of this just fine," Justin said. "That is what Tommy wanted, wasn't it? Sure enough, we're going to be simply fine when this is over."

"Wait," Dana said. She looked up at the tiles of the hung ceiling. "Do you hear that?"

"Yup," Justin said. "He's up on the roof again."

"Maybe we could make a run for it," she said. "We might be able to find the rest of the crew."

"No way," Justin said. "Between that asshole on the roof and whoever is in the wheelhouse, we'd be goners as soon as we opened this door, for sure."

"We've got to do something."

"We've got to stay alive," Justin said. "You heard all the shooting that's been going on. We might be the only ones left."

They were both taken by surprise when the boat's crazy motion stopped. Someone who knew how to steer a boat had taken control, and the *Nighthawk* was steaming steadily through the fog once again.

"Tom must be okay!" Dana said.

But Justin shook his head, and he said, "I doubt that."

The growler phone next to the door buzzed. Justin picked up the handset. "Who's this?" he said. After a few seconds he turned to Dana. "It's Bo," Justin said. "He's got Todd with him in the engine room. They have taken control down there to steer for Hyannis, and he wants us to keep an eye out up here. What do you think?"

"That sounds good to me," Dana said. "Except that we cannot see anything ahead, only what's behind the boat. And not much there, with this fog."

Justin conferred with Bo on the phone again, and they decided that at least he and Dana could let them know if help arrived, or if they passed some landmark or buoy close enough to be seen through the fog, or if their situation changed in some other way. Then, in mid-sentence, Justin looked out the window and said, "No! Damn it! No!"

Dana went to the one-way window over the food prep counter and saw that Lou was coming up the stairway from the promenade. Grant was right behind him. They were showing their heads above the rim of the stairway, about a hundred feet away from the shooter, who had a rifle with a telescopic sight on the roof of the galley. "No!" She pounded on the glass. "Go back!" she yelled. "Go back!"

They would not hear her over the distance and the sound of the engines echoing from the smokestack.

The Ladies' Room

The young woman with dreadlocks took a push broom with a heavy handle from Helen. She hefted it and quickly unscrewed the brush, leaving the handle alone as a nimbler and more effective weapon. She was a short, busty woman with obvious athletic ability. "I'm Brianna," she said. Her eyes were dark and alert. "Let's do this."

"Yes," Helen said. "We'll do whatever we have to do."

Brianna calmly nodded in agreement, and Helen knew that she had a formidable ally to protect their shelter from intrusion.

"What is going to happen?" a woman holding a toddler said. Other women clutched their children in terror and looked to Helen for answers.

"Don't worry," Helen said. "No one is going to get through that door."

"Amen, sister," Brianna said.

"Let's take stock of our situation," Helen said, while she rummaged through the cleaning supplies in the closet and came out with a yellow half-gallon squeeze bottle.

"Be careful with that bottle," Brianna said. "That's acidic toilet bowl cleaner."

At that moment, a stall door opened and a distinguished-looking woman with coiffed gray hair emerged from the end toilet. She blinked and looked at the women and children who had not been there when she went into the stall. "Oh my," she meekly said. "What is happening?"

"It's okay," Helen said. "There's trouble on the boat. We're safe in here."

"Trouble? What trouble?"

"There is a shooter on the loose," Helen said. "If we remain quiet, we'll be okay in here until the danger passes."

"No," the woman said. "No, no! My husband. I have to be with my husband."

"Your husband will be fine," Helen said. "They all went to the cocktail lounge."

"No," the woman said, bolting for the door. "My husband!"

Brianna barred the woman's path. "Take it easy," she said. "You're upsetting the children."

Other women said, "Sit down and shut up."

"No, my husband. We have been married fifty-one years. I have grown children of my own, and grandchildren. I have to be with him."

"Don't you see?" Helen said. "This isn't about you. Or your husband, or me. This is about these children. Your leaving could tip off our hiding spot. We can't risk that."

Helen's heart swelled when Teddy came out from under the sinks and took the woman by the hand. "It's okay," he said. "My father won't let anything bad happen to us."

"That's right," Ricky said, cradling Olivia in his arms under the sinks. "You'll see, our father will take care of the bad men."

10

RECONNAISANCE

The Game Room

Before Grant and Lou were out of sight on their mission to retake the wheelhouse, Sean left the game room and began scavenging through the personal articles that some passengers had left behind on nearby seats.

"What are you doing?" Damien said. "This is no time for looting."

"I don't give a crap about this stuff," Sean said, tossing a man's jacket aside. "I'm looking for something useful. There must be a ladies' handbag somewhere around here."

"There's one," Damien said, pointing to an expensive-looking tote on a nearby seat. "But—"

"Perfect," Sean said as he reached the Louis Vuitton bag and dumped the contents on the floor. He pushed aside the hairbrush, the wallet, and the Kotex, and focused on one small item—a folding powder compact. "Estee Lauder," Sean said as he held up the container with an ornate faux-jewel design on the cover. "Probably two hundred bucks at Neiman Marcus."

Damien thought that the cop might have gone berserk when he twisted the cover off the compact and tossed the powder and applicator aside. Until Sean turned the small round mirror inside the cover toward him and said, "This part is priceless right now."

"I get it," Damien said, looking at his own reflection in the mirror. "That's how we see around corners."

Sean scampered back to the game room when they heard two shots—*Crack! Crack!* —from above. "I hope to Hell that was Lou shooting," Damien said.

"There's no way to tell," Sean said. "Unless our guys don't come back."

They counted the moments and seconds after that. Damien forgot to breathe until Grant and Lou retreated around the corner from the stairway, and he said, "Thank God."

"That's not going to work," Grant said, as he knelt on the deck in the game room with Damien and Sean. "There's a sniper on the roof of the galley."

"He's got the high ground," Lou said. The old fisherman crouched low and spoke over his shoulder from a defensive posture alongside Sean at the door to the game room, in case they had been followed. "That asshole has a scope on his weapon. He opened up as soon as I showed my head at the top of the stairs. I couldn't even get a shot off."

They hardly noticed that the boat's rolling motion had subsided. Someone had taken control to steer a steady course through the fog. To where, was the question.

"Lou, your cheek is bleeding," Damien said. Small trickles of blood were seeping from what looked like scrapes below his eye.

"That's okay," Lou said. "That son-of-a-bitch dropped his first round short and wide of his target—my big fat head—when I popped up to look. That is just some crap the bullet kicked up as it ricocheted off the deck and went by my ear. Lucky for us he does not know shit about combat. If he had stayed in cover and waited until we were out in the open on the sundeck—well, we wouldn't be here."

"We can forget getting to the radio in the wheelhouse," Grant said. "And my portable radio is on the charger in my stateroom right now, which is right behind the wheelhouse."

"What now?" Damien said.

"I don't know," Grant said. "Lou, what do you think?"

"Hell, if I know, Grant. My job in 'Nam was to be out on point and shoot Charlie before he shot me, while the rest of the platoon maneuvered up to finish them off. I've never even thought about a hostage thing."

"Well, officer," Grant said, looking at Sean. "I guess it's up to you."

"I'm staying right here," Sean said. "My family is behind that door to the ladies' room, so I'll deal with these assholes if they come this way. But if I was on the job—unless there was an active shooter—I'd set up a perimeter and call in the Emergency Services Unit. They'd show up with the assault teams, snipers, and hostage negotiators. Even the bomb squad, and they would deal with it. I don't know what to tell you, Captain."

"What if there was an active shooter?"

"Jeez," Sean said. "If they are shooting people, we go in—we just go in—that's the cop's nightmare. We go in with whatever we have, not what we wish we had, even if it doesn't end well."

"Count me in," Lou said.

"Not so fast," Grant said. "What was that about a perimeter?"

"That's pretty much where you're at," Sean said. "Contain the situation and come up with a plan. Only at the present time, we're the ones who are contained."

"Good," Grant said. "I like that. I have been going over this in my mind, and I think we need to take a minute to figure out what we are up against. It is those five guys who came aboard in that heavy-duty pickup truck with Michigan plates, isn't it? Just five of them."

"We're down to four," Damien said. "Thanks to Lou."

"Right," Grant said. "Now, if one of them is in the wheelhouse, and another is on top of the galley covering the sundeck, there must only be two guys holding the passengers hostage. And there are four of us."

"Two guys with body armor and assault weapons," Sean said.

"That's fair," Grant said. "Now what about our crew?"

"Saint is down," Lou said. "And Tom is, you know—"

Sean said, "An old black man—I think he is the engineer—dragged the young kid from the car deck into the engine room while I was down there. The kid got clobbered while the perps were taking weapons out of their vehicle."

"Good," Grant said. "Now we know where Bo and Todd are. And I am quite sure that Justin and Dana are locked into the galley. So that leaves Dylan and Butch unaccounted for. But they are smart guys, and only about half of the passengers are in the lounge, so I am going to bet that Dylan and Butch are hiding the rest of them somewhere. Does that sound about right?"

"Sure," Lou said. "What's next?"

"Maybe we can talk to their leader," Grant said.

"I like that idea," Damien said. "We don't even know who these guys are, or what they want. Let's find some answers."

"No, talking to these guys is a terrible idea," Sean said. "Trained negotiators always talk from a position of power, when the perps are surrounded by a phalanx of heavily armed cops, with helicopters overhead. We are outgunned here, if you didn't notice. Any untrained talker would fall for the Stockholm syndrome in a moment, and the bad guys would own you."

"Maybe," Grant said. "Lou, what do you think?"

"You know how I think," Lou said. "We shouldn't show our hand until we have an advantage. I say we take them by surprise."

"Damien?"

"I still want to know who they are and what they want. Fact is, we can't negotiate until we know what's on the table."

Grant considered the three opinions from the cop, the combat veteran, and the businessman: One, do not talk and wait for law enforcement. Or two, start shooting. Or maybe the third way was to negotiate terms. What really surprised him was that he seemed to be starting with a blank slate, with no strong opinion of his own. "The way I see it, we have to do something," Grant said. "Sooner or later they are going to come looking for the rest of the passengers. And by now, they must be missing the guy Lou threw over the side. They'll come looking for him, too."

"They probably haven't figured out that I took that asshole's AK," Lou said. "I never got a chance to show it on the sundeck."

"So, if we don't negotiate, we only have two choices," Grant said. "Do we go after them first? Or do we try to pick them off one at a time when they come looking for us?"

"Either way, it's a bad scene for the hostages when the shooting starts," Sean said. "Let's take it down the middle and get close enough to the lounge to see what's going on in there. Then we'll know."

"I'm in," Lou said. "Recon is my life."

Grant said, "Then I guess it's me and you again, Lou."

"No," Sean said. "I should go with Lou."

"That is great," Grant said. "But I thought you were staying by the door to the ladies' room."

"I am," Sean said. "But I can't let this old soldier do this alone."

"We should all go," Damien said.

"No way," Sean said. "The four of us will never get in and out without being noticed. The plan is to get close enough to look and come right back." He turned to Lou. "You know the boat a lot better than me, so if you go on point, I'll have your back."

The Forward Passenger Compartment

Sean looked around the half-opened fire door with his mirror when he and Lou huddled in the hallway outside the game room, ready to go into the forward compartment.

"You know," Sean said. "I've been doing some math. A man who was in Saigon for the Tet offensive would have to be at least seventy years old. Are you sure you're up for this?"

"Ha!" Lou said. "I'm worried that you're too young for this. Your mind is on your family behind that ladies' room door, not the enemy. That could get us both killed."

"I'm only thinking about one thing now, old-timer. How are we going to do this?"

"The entrance to the lounge is on the starboard side, so we'll keep as low and close to the booths on the port side as we can. Are you ready?"

"Go," Sean said. Lou moved like a cat, staying low. They moved from booth to booth, chair to chair, until they reached the delicatessen.

Lou crept into a booth near the food service counter and the entrance to the cocktail lounge and kneeled under the table. Sean followed and dropped to a prone position. They were close enough then to smell the odor of caged humanity—the sick and the terrified—as Sean used the mirror to look inside the chamber of misery. He moved the compact mirror slowly and purposefully, knowing that any sudden or jittery movements of the reflective glass would draw attention like a beacon.

He could only see the area closest to the entrance, but that was enough. There was a man—a crewman, by his blue trousers—down in a pool of blood, with an armed man standing above the body. The shooter's left side was closest to the door, and Sean recognized him as the attacker who had taken the first action, by snatching the inept security man's handgun. The handgun was nowhere in sight, but there was now an AK-47 assault rifle with a folding stock across the man's chest, which was sheathed in body armor.

There was a woman close to the shooter's right side, partially obscured from view by the man's bulk. What Sean saw next sent a shiver down his spine—the shooter had rigged a kill-noose and a sawed-off shotgun round the woman's neck. Her tight capris pants and the flash of silk around her neck were unmistakable. This was the woman who had served his coffee a little more than three-quarters of an hour earlier. The subdued smile and soft "thank you" she had offered when he slipped a dollar bill into her tip jar flashed through his mind.

In the same instant Sean saw her eyes shift his way.

She looked past the shooter and spotted his tiny mirror, close to the floor, twenty feet away. Sean held his breath and kept the compact mirror rock steady. The glance lasted little more than a breathless second before she looked back at the shooter without betraying his position.

"Good girl," Sean whispered to himself, when her expression remained unchanged and she did not give a second glance. There was no doubt that she had seen them, and that her mind had processed the fact of their presence with extraordinary alacrity.

This woman was a survivor.

Sean slowly tilted the mirror slightly toward his own shoulder so that Lou could see into the lounge. The old soldier made a pistol sign with his forefinger and pointed it at the shooter. Then he pressed his finger against his own forehead, silently signaling, *I can take him out with a headshot.*

Sean shook his head, *no.*

The Cocktail Lounge

Katarina felt much better when the boat's violent rocking subsided. The stale air in the lounge had become fetid with the repugnant smells of seasickness and fear, but she no longer felt the terror that had risen in her chest each time the deck under their feet had shifted—knowing that the man's finger on the trigger of the shotgun wired to her neck might slip at any time—until she choked the bile back down. At least now, with the slippery deck underfoot calmed, she had the hope of living another minute. Then another. And another.

Any hope, however, seemed thin. The other masked man—the shorter and heavier one who had been called Stumpy—was nervously training his assault rifle around the room and speaking gibberish peppered with vile threats. When she glanced down, Katarina saw that the deck under her feet was lubricated with an expanding pool of Tony's blood. But she choked the bile down again when she saw something else out of the corner of her eye.

What is that?

For an instant she thought it was a passenger in hiding in a nearby booth. Her heart had few precious beats to skip, so she never lost her composure and quickly looked away. Somebody was spying on them, and the fear that they might try something rash was again a palpable mass rising in her chest. Yet there was a chance—a very slim chance—that these peeping toms might have their wits about them. She knew that her only hope was to ignore them and to focus on this horrible man holding her at the slippery precipice of eternity.

And she prayed.

She noticed the big man in coveralls coming down the stairway from the sundeck. He would pass close to the spies when he came in from the promenade, so she held her head high and dared not to look that way for fear that her eyes might drop and betray the presence of the spies as he entered this purgatory.

"Good job getting the boat under control," the leader said. "I knew I could count on you, Behr."

"Hell no," the bearded giant said, almost slipping in Tony's blood. "Zack isn't steering this thing now—he's still spinning the wheel—but he's so stupid he doesn't know that what he's doing isn't worth a shit. Somebody else is driving this boat."

"What?" the leader said. Katarina felt the wire around her neck tighten when he tensed and became agitated. Her father and brothers had kept similar firearms for hunting, so she knew that the knurled thumb-slide above the triggers was the safety. The red dot showing meant that the gun could fire at the slightest provocation. The urge to reach up and slide the safety on when her tormenter was not looking was nearly overpowering, but his index finger was inside the trigger guard. Any movement she made might be fatal.

"It's got to be somebody in the engine room," Behr said.

"Then goddamn do something about it," the leader said. "While you're down there tell Colt to get his ass up here, pronto."

"Don't sweat it, Matthias," the big man said. "I can handle this."

Katarina allowed herself to exhale a deep breath when Behr went out the door to the promenade not far from the spies without seeing them. What was more, she now knew the leader's name. He had been called Matthias. That was something.

"Now, you," Matthias said. He pointed his assault rifle at another woman among the hostages. At first Katarina believed that he was singling out a woman in Muslim garb, holding an infant. But Stumpy stepped toward the terrified people and pushed a few men aside to grab a different young woman, who gasped and put her hand on the small Star of David pendant she wore around her neck. Stumpy pulled her out of the group while a young man clutched her in a vain attempt to hold her back.

"No, take me instead," Ezra said. He stepped in front of his dearest, only to get knocked to his knees by the butt of Stump's rifle.

"Take it easy," some men said as they pulled him back into the group. "You'll get us all killed."

The men held Ezra back while Stumpy dragged Abbey to Matthias, who took the terrified woman's pendant in his hand and said, "I knew I smelled a Jewess in the room."

Abbey's mouth was moving but paralyzing fear had robbed her of breath and words. Inches away, Katarina fought through her own fear to speak. "Time to be brave," Katarina said. "We're going to be all right, just do as they say."

"You shut up," Matthias said, growling and tugging hard on the kill-noose around Katarina's neck. "Remember rule one? Speak when spoken to."

"Is this one mine?" Stumpy said. As soon as Matthias agreed, Stumpy pulled an identical shotgun and wire noose from his hip pack. Abbey sobbed and stood with her hands at her side and her head bowed while the short man looped the kill-noose around her neck. He then produced a roll of black duct tape from his pack, and took several turns of it around his left hand and the grip of the shotgun, firmly affixing his grasp on the weapon—and to the hostage captured in his noose.

Stumpy offered the tape to Matthias. He said, "Want some of this for that bitch's mouth?"

"No," Matthias said. "Use that on the Jewess."

"How about a little kiss first," Stumpy said. Katarina recoiled when he leaned close to Abbey and pulled the ski mask off his head, exposing a warty face with crude prison tattoos and horrendously bad teeth.

Abbey fainted before this troll of her nightmares. Stumpy grabbed her by the neck with his free hand. He held her up and said, "Stand up, you stupid bitch! I almost blew your head off."

"You made her faint," Katarina said.

"You shut up," Matthias said as he jerked the shotgun and the wire noose around Katarina's neck. "Your next words will be your last."

Stumpy was fumbling with the roll of duct tape, confronting the realization that he would not be able to cover Abbey's mouth with one hand while the other was taped to the shotgun, when a skinny blonde teenager walked into the lounge. Katarina's first thought was that the youth was a disoriented passenger who had stumbled into the scene— he looked so innocent—until she saw that he too carried an assault rifle.

"Where the hell have you been?" Matthias said.

"I was guarding the truck," the boy answered. "Some guy got close and broke into the van behind us, but I stayed out of sight. Nobody got near our truck."

"Forget about the truck," Matthias said. "You should have come up when you heard the shooting."

"Colt," Stumpy said. "Now that you are here, give me a hand, boy. Cover this bitch's mouth so I don't have to listen to her Jew words."

"Sure," Colt said. He was exploding with bravado when let his rifle hang from the combat sling to take the duct-tape from Stumpy. "Are we going to take turns with her?"

Until Matthias said, "Shut up, Colt. That's not how we treat prisoners of war on the field of battle—we wait until after the trials."

Katarina studied the teenager as he ripped off a length of the tape. He was still leering when he held it up in front of Abbey's face. Until he was close to her. Inches away, he hesitated, and his features softened. He was no longer bold. He was afraid. *There is still humanity in that boy*, Katarina thought.

"Get it done," Matthias said.

The boy almost seemed to cry as he looked at the helpless woman, but he said, "Yes, sir," and pressed the tape onto Abbey's mouth.

"You better get serious, boy," Matthias said. "This mission is real now. Remember your training. Get over here and take control of this shotgun."

"Please put the safety on," Katarina said when Matthias transferred his grip on the shotgun to the boy. But the leader rebuffed her again and took the roll of tape from Stumpy. Katarina looked into the boy's eyes while Matthias used the tape to take several turns around the boy's wrist and the butt of the weapon wired to her neck. His eyes were pale gray, like Matthias's, and she realized that there was some relation there. It pained her to think that his soft, youthful features might someday harden into a hateful mask such as his elder's. "It's okay," she softly said while Matthias wound the tape. "It's okay."

"Stumpy, don't just stand there," Matthias said. "Go find Hunter. And round up any of these sheep that are hiding."

"Where should I look?"

"His post was at the back of the boat. Start there."

"Okay," Stumpy said. "No problem." He positioned Abbey in front of himself and pushed her toward the delicatessen and the forward passenger compartment. As they passed Katarina made eye contact with the other woman's pleading eyes and she nodded, *it is going to be okay.* Even though things were anything but okay, as Stumpy pushed her ahead of himself and called for Hunter, looking around corners and under tables.

She held her breath when Stumpy got to the booth where she had seen the peeping tom's tiny mirror—and exhaled when he looked under that table and kept moving. She wondered who it had been, and she thought about Damien and hoped he would survive these horrible events. She looked at the face of her young captor and realized that if this boy did not slip and kill her by accident, he would do whatever Matthias commanded, without hesitation. Matthias had all the answers. He was more than a fanatic; he was a messiah to this boy.

My fate is now in the hand of a confused teenager and his mad-dog messiah, she thought. *And God. Do not forget God.*

The Game Room

"We saw four shooters," Sean said when he and Lou were back in the game room with Grant and Damien. "The leader is named Matthias."

"That's right," Lou said. "The piece of shit who shot Saint was crying for Matthias at the end."

Sean said, "While we were watching, Matthias and a fat little man were holding the passengers at gunpoint, and the third one—a kid they called Colt—came up from the freight deck. He walked right past without seeing us. The big man with all the hair came down from above while we were watching, too."

"What are we really up against?" Damien said. "There are more bad guys than the five who came aboard in the pickup truck. The question is, how many more?"

"That kid might have been driving the deli truck that came on last,"

Grant said. "That would make sense, since I think his passenger was a guy named Zack Brody, who worked in our deli for a short time."

"I remember Zack," Damien said. "If I had known that little punk was here again, I would have kicked his puny ass off our property."

"That cocky little shit thought he knew all about boats," Lou said. "He might be the one who was giving us the wild ride if he tried to take the helm."

"We're steadied up now," Sean said. "Is the boat on autopilot?"

"None of our boats have autopilots," Damien said. "Somebody has to have their hands on the helm at all times. If you let go while the engines are at full power, the boat will just wrap up into a tighter and tighter turn, even with the rudder amidships."

"I don't think someone in the wheelhouse has control," Grant said. "I'm betting that Bo took local control in the engine room. He and Todd have to be steering us back to the mainland."

"Of course," Damien said. "The bad guys might not have figured that out yet."

"There's something else," Lou said. "Tony is a goner. There's a lot of blood on the deck."

"So, that was the shot we heard," Grant said.

"Damn it," Damien said. "We really needed the strongman to get out of this mess."

"You can say that again," Grant said. "Saint and Tony were our two linebackers. This is going to be a lot harder without them."

"I have more bad news," Sean said. "They have a wire kill-noose rigged up to a shotgun around a woman's neck. That is not something they put together on the spur of the moment. These perps came prepared for a kidnapping."

"Ugh," Grant said. "Now I am sure they were going to attack the Nantucket Conference, until we had to turn around. Any one of those high-tech billionaires would have been a fat prize. Too bad we didn't have some warning."

"What woman?" Damien said, with an extra edge of tension in his words.

"It's Katarina," Lou said. "Tough break, Damien. I could have taken the leader with a head shot, but she might not have made it."

"That's still an option," Sean said. "It might be your only choice, if the cavalry doesn't arrive soon."

"No," Damien said. "We're not going to do it that way. There has to be a way to make a deal with these people."

"Katarina?" Sean said. "Isn't that the girl who served my coffee in the snack bar? What is going on here?"

Damien said, "Katarina is—my—she is important."

"Your girlfriend?"

"More than a girlfriend," Damien said. "She's going to be my wife—after we get clear of this mess."

"Congratulations," Sean said. "I have to tell you that your bride's only chance is a hostage negotiator with serious skills."

"I am a negotiator with serious skills," Damien said. "One thing you learn in business at my level is that you can make a deal with anyone when you have to. We were not the first target of these people, so let's find out what they really want. That's where we start the bidding."

"They could have gotten a king's ransom for one of those high-tech billionaires at the conference," Grant said.

"Damien, I can tell you exactly what they want," Sean said. "They want to make a statement, and that statement is that they hate rich boys like you. You are one of the people screwing everything up. What you call business as usual is oppression to them, so forget about talking. They do not make a statement by dying, they make it by killing you. Don't you get that? The only thing that will save your bride—maybe— is an overwhelming show of force."

"That's right," Lou said. "The only way they will give up now is if they think they can live to fight another day."

"Okay, let's find a better position and regroup," Grant said. "Bo is saving the day right now." He held up his cell phone. "I almost have a service bar on my phone, so if he keeps us on course for Hyannis, we'll be out of the dead zone soon, and help will be on the way, for sure."

"Now you're talking," Sean said. "They will come looking back here very soon, so your best bet is to get into a concealed position to monitor what's going on in the lounge. That way if things get out of hand before the reinforcements arrive, Lou can do his thing."

"I don't want to fight them in this passageway when they come looking for us," Grant said. "We need to find a better location."

"Right," Lou said, hefting the AK-47. "Let's outflank them. I think we should go down and head toward the bow on the 'tween decks. We can stay low and out of sight behind cars and come up on the forward stairs, right next to the lounge."

"That sounds like the best plan," Grant said. "The bow is the place to be with our cell phones—we want as little steel as possible between us and the towers on the Cape. And we can take a page out of Sean's book and pull a few sideview mirrors off cars on the way, so we can see around corners."

"Anything is better than sitting here waiting," Damien said.

"Okay," Lou said. "Follow me. We'll go down the aft stairs." The older man turned back to Sean, and he said," Are you sure you don't want in on this? We could really use another gun."

"I'd ride the river with you anytime, old-timer," Sean said. "But that's my family in there. Good luck."

The Ladies' Room

Helen climbed onto a countertop to peer through the grille of a vent near the ceiling in the ladies' room. She caught a glimpse of her husband across the hall in the game room and heard his parting words to the others when they left. When she whispered, "Please come in here," Sean raised his index finger to his lips to hush her and then held up his palm, *wait*. Then he sank back into the shadows of the game room, out of sight.

A few minutes later she heard someone approaching from the forward compartment. "Hunter!" a man said as he approached. "Where the hell are you? Get out here."

Helen shrank from the vent when a squat, ugly man came into sight—*a repulsive beast*, Helen thought—pushing a woman ahead. The woman's head was bowed in a mask of panic and tears—but—that was Abbey! And the beast was holding some sort of gun to her neck. He had a pistol in his other hand and an assault rifle hanging loosely by a sling at his chest.

Sean, do something! Helen thought. But he shrank into the shadows in the game room as the beast and his hostage passed into the aft passenger compartment.

The beast was excited and more dragging than pushing Abbey when he came back to the hallway. He stood in the half open fire door and yelled into the forward compartment. "Hey! Hey, Colt!" the beast said. "There's a dead guy outside, but no sign of Hunter."

The answer came from someone out of sight. "Stumpy, you dope," a young voice said. "Matthias said to check the bathrooms."

"Yeah, okay," the beast named Stumpy said. Helen watched as he went to the men's room across the hall and pushed the door open. It slammed against the wall at the end of a full swing. "Hey!" Stumpy yelled. "Get the hell out of here. Yeah, you! Now!" He glared at the people who came out of hiding, threatening with his pistol. "Get in the cocktail lounge with everybody else," he said.

The people who had been hiding in the men's room hung their heads and complied with Stumpy's demands. There was at least a dozen of them who marched to the cocktail lounge like sheep. What else could they do, when confronted by a man with a gun?

"This is it," Helen said, when she dropped down from the vent. "He will come here next." Brianna was leaning toward the door. "Bring it on," she said, hefting her broom handle. Her dreadlocks and beads swung as she twisted her head to loosen her neck muscles.

Helen took the other broom handle in her hands and stood alongside Brianna. She turned to the other women and said, "If we go down, don't give up. Resist!" But her words were met with fearful, blank stares that made her realize that this battle would be won or lost with the two of them at the door.

The door banged open a few inches and hit the trash can. For two seconds nothing happened. Then Stumpy said, "What the hell?" He tried to force the door open again before he stuck his head in the crack to look inside.

The first thrust of Brianna's broom handle landed on his cheek. He reeled, and she hit him again in the neck. "You stupid bitch!" Stumpy said. He thrust his pistol through the crack and tried to aim it at Brianna, but Helen aimed her broom handle at his privates and thrust hard. Brianna was up on top of the trash barrel by then, with a leg up, pushing on the door. Then she had her back against the partition with both legs jamming the door shut. Stump's arm was down and stuck in the door. He could not raise the pistol to fire at Helen. She grabbed the squeeze bottle of industrial toilet bowl cleaner and sent a stream of the sticky acid into his face and eyes.

The beast squealed in agony.

The door opened fully when the trash barrel shifted, and Brianna fell to the floor. Stump's wailing continued as he burst into the ladies' room—pushed by Sean—who had come from behind to grab Stumpy's fingers away from the trigger of the shotgun wired to Abbey's neck. He bent them backward until the index finger was pointed back at Stumpy's face. The beast squealed in panic as Sean spun him and pushed his squat form backward into the ladies' room, attacking so swiftly that Stumpy never had a chance to fire a shot or call for help. He held him against the partition and beat his face and forehead mercilessly with the pipe he had taken from Todd—once, twice—five times, until he had partially lobotomized the beast.

Abbey collapsed with Stumpy when he slumped to the floor. Sean quickly unraveled the tape that held the beast's hand to the shotgun. He pulled the duct-tape from her mouth and gently lifted her limp form toward Helen's outstretched arms. "Ezra," she said, barely conscious. "I've got to get to Ezra."

"I'll help Ezra," Sean said. "You stay in here."

"Sean," Helen said, pleading. "Stay in here with us."

"This isn't over," he said. He dragged Stump's limp form across the hall toward the game room. "That was only round one. Pick up his pistol off the floor and remember what I told you—if you have to use it, keep shooting until the enemy is down and stops moving."

MANIFESTO

The Cocktail Lounge

L isten up, people," Matthias said, standing on the bar. "This is the great American awakening. This is the start of a new civil war that will mark the end of the Deep State. We The People are taking Our Land back for the rightful owners, the White Race—our blood and our soil. The future belongs to the strong. None of you will be hurt if you all do as you're told, but you must obey and learn—you must learn the truths that have been hidden from you by the Zionist Occupied Government."

"Blood and soil," Colt said, chanting and slipping deeper into a self-hypnotic state with each refrain. "Blood and soil." The boy stood between the hostages and the exit, with one hand on the shotgun at Katarina's throat, tugging on the wire noose around her neck with each verse. *Blood and soil.*

"You must learn to recognize your true enemies," Matthias said. "The same powerful elites who control the politicians and the news media also control your entertainment and the contents of your wallets. Money is their god, and liberal lies are the venom they use to control your thoughts and actions. One by one, they have taken away our freedoms and empowered their Zionist courts to overturn our home rules and our God-given rights. The Globalist agenda is to achieve total control of the world with one eternal fascist government that will be the culmination of history's progress. Hear me, people! This is the evil goal of the New World Order! History will mark this moment—"

A loud fart interrupted Matthias's speech. "In this glorious hour—" He stumbled over his words before he regained his fervor. "In this glorious hour we shall rise up," Matthias said. "This is the beginning of the civil war that will overthrow the one percent who would enslave us with the witchcraft of their Bretton Woods Agreement. We must become unreasonable to throw off the yoke of oppression that channels all the fruits of our labors into their high temple of wealth on Wall Street. In this glorious hour we shall fight back. Our first mission is to abolish the fake news media so that only the truth can be told. Millions of true patriots will take up arms against the elites when they see what we have achieved this day. We The People will use whatever force is necessary to make the liars of the fake news media afraid to show their faces. In this glorious hour—"

Another long offensive rip interrupted Matthias. He stumbled on the well-rehearsed words of his lecture, obviously confused as to the source of the rude emissions, which seemed to emanate from behind the bar.

So, the leader is not as phlegmatic as he pretends to be, Katarina thought. *He can be distracted. This false messiah can be made to veer off course.*

Matthias stepped down off the bar and kicked the door of the broom closet behind the bar, eliciting a pitiful whimper from within. "You! Get out," he said. "Come out and stand before me!" He kicked the door again. "This flimsy door will not protect you. Come out and join us."

The portly security man emerged from the niche with torrents of sweat soaking his face and shirt. Judd cowered more than stood in front of Matthias, bowing and begging for his next breath. "Please, you can't shoot me—I'm unarmed—I was just doing my job—I—I—have a family—I—"

He had peed in his pants.

Judd was so pathetic in that moment that Katarina found pity for him in her soul, even though he had squandered the hiding place where she had meant to provide refuge to some innocent children early in the attack.

"You were the first to oppose our glorious movement," Matthias said. His words regained their pseudo-majestic cadence as he spoke them. "This treason will be judged by a military court in a time of battle. How say ye, members of the jury?"

"Guilty!" Colt said, without hesitation. "Guilty. Guilty!"

"And what shall the judgment for treason be?"

Katarina studied her young captor while his attention was riveted on Matthias. The youth was mesmerized by his leader, in waves of near ecstasy. She wondered if there might be a moment between the waves when she might reason with him, an emotional lull in which she could reach up and engage the shotgun's safety mechanism herself, if he was unwilling to do so. That moment would not come while Matthias was on his high horse, she knew. While immersed in his leader's oratory, this boy, this unfinished human being, was becoming a monster.

"Death!" Colt said. "Death to all traitors!"

"So be it," Matthias said. "The jury has spoken." Katarina saw joy in Colt's features, as if Matthias's vacuous words carried some actual moral authority. As if unrestrained confidence and grandiose eloquence made the murder that was about to occur a legitimate act. A moral imperative, even. The one trait that all fanatics share, she knew, was the absolute belief that their own personal experiences and perceptions are the ground truth of a global reality. That they alone see the issues clearly, that their logic is the only pure path to the final truth. That they will latch on to any convoluted theory that reinforces their fallacy while disarming facts by impeaching the sources. These things Katarina, as an educated and thoughtful European woman, understood as the foundational lessons of history.

What mystified her was why some people persist—to this day—in siphoning such overt insanity into themselves, as if to fill the empty corners in their own souls.

The crescendo of Judd's sobbing blather came when Matthias brandished a large chrome revolver. This was the weapon he had taken from Judd. "Judgment having been passed, it is decreed that the traitor should die by his own weapon." The doomed man's pleading were indecipherable snorts by then. Katarina's own predicament was nearly forgotten in that moment, overshadowed by irrepressible compassion. With pity that Judd would be a soulless pauper in the end, bankrupt of grace in the hour of his death. He tried to squirm away. Matthias pressed the defrocked security man's flabby bulk against the wall behind the bar, toppling the few remaining bottles of liquor from the shelves. Judd grabbed at the barrel of his own gun and tried to push it away with hands that were weak with panic. Matthias pressed the muzzle between his eyes and pulled the trigger. The top of Judd's head, an indistinct blob of his blood and bone and brains, splatted against the mirror behind the bar in an instant, before the dull report of the large-caliber ammunition—the sound and the palpable shock wave—rippled through the air.

Colt's jaw dropped. Katarina seized the moment of his distraction to reach up and grasp his forearm with both hands. He turned to her and she met his eyes. She locked onto his soul and began the most meaningful dance of her life. Panic erupted in the bar lounge. People were fleeing, pushing past her and Colt to reach the exit. A mob roiled around them, pushing and slipping and shoving past them. She held Colt's eyes with her own. Nothing around them mattered. A blur. They were alone in the crowd, joined in a slow pirouette, bumped and jostled by the stream of humanity rushing past them. They made two full turns, carried in the current, before he let his rifle hang from the sling across his chest and reached for her. His hand was on hers when she moved it up his forearm and they reached the safety together. His pale eyes seemed lost. He could not refuse her. They engaged the safety together. They remained connected by the shotgun taped to his wrist and the noose encircling her neck. Yet Katarina sensed in his defenseless eyes that he would not harm her. She said thank you with her eyes at the same moment that Matthias reached them and began pushing them too, shoving Colt toward the exit. "Go!" the leader said. "Go! Go!" They let the mob carry them out of the lounge. There the rush of former hostages bifurcated, with half exiting through the door to the promenade and others gushing into the forward passenger deck.

Katarina and Colt were still connected by the shotgun taped to his wrist and the noose around her neck when they pirouetted in unison one more time where the stream of humanity divided. At least the safety was on so that her death would have to be an intentional act. She looked away from the boy's eyes only long enough to see Damien and Grant rising from hiding on the bow to smash the picture windows at the front of the lounge with red fire axes. They leapt through shattering glass into the lounge, followed by more crewmen in their blue uniforms, pushing scattered chairs and frightened passengers aside. The rescuers came in hot pursuit while Matthias pushed Colt and Katarina deeper into the fleeing crowd.

The Forecastle

Lou had led Grant and Damien to the bow via the portside 'tween deck, where small cars were parked in a tight bond above the freight deck. They pulled sideview mirrors off cars on the way, and Grant and Damien took the axes from fire stations, which they now hefted as lethal weapons. They encountered Dylan in the dark shadows as they neared the bow. "Ain't this some crazy shit?" he said, when he saw the fire axes they held. "Are you guys going medieval, or what?" Then he told them of the passengers that he and Butch had secreted in the lower cargo hold.

Now a foursome, they went up to the forecastle, where the mooring and anchor handling gear was located. They had initially taken positions ahead of the heavy steel bulwark of the spray shield, being careful not to go as far forward as the anchor windlass, which could be seen from the wheelhouse. From there they were able to use their mirrors like periscopes to see into the bar lounge, with mist and spray flying over their heads, since Bo and Todd were still steaming the *Nighthawk* toward Hyannis at full speed, blindly through the fog.

"We need to be closer," Grant said, crouching behind the steel barrier. "Damien, do you think you and I can get right under the windows to the cocktail lounge without being sighted?" Damien nodded. Then

125

Grant turned to Lou and Dylan. "You can cover us from here, Lou. We will be too close to use these mirrors to look inside without being spotted. If they start harming passengers in the lounge, just give a yell, and Damien and I will break the windows with our axes. Then we can all jump in. If we're lucky, we'll take them totally by surprise."

"Now you're talking," Lou said.

"Sounds good," Dylan said. He stayed low and picked up a heavy iron pike, which on a normal day the deckhands would use to twist and unkink the anchor chain. "I'm getting tired of hiding from these jerkwads."

The promenade extended all around the passenger deck to include an open area for sightseers ahead of the picture windows of the bar lounge. Grant and Damien went around the spray shield, playing the blind spots at the corners of the lounge, and crouched there, under windows that faced the bow.

Grant stayed low and spring-loaded for action. He looked at his cell phone and was disappointed to see that he did not yet have even a glimmer of service, even though the boat was getting closer to the Cape with each passing minute. When he saw the time shown on the device, he thought that the phone might have stopped working altogether. Could it possibly be true that only twenty-six minutes had elapsed from the time when Tom turned the boat around? That did not make any sense. It seemed that the ordeal had lasted for hours. Would it ever end?

He tried to block the nagging doubts from his thoughts. Had he missed an opportunity to evacuate the passengers into the life rafts? That would not have been possible while the attackers took the *Nighthawk* on that rollicking wild joyride, like a whaleboat on a Nantucket Sleigh Ride. Thank God that was over! Yet he knew that even if the vessel were stopped dead in the water the passengers would have been easy targets in the rafts.

No, Grant decided. Keeping the passengers in the boat had been the only possible course of action. If only he could see a few bars on his cell phone, help might arrive in time to save this day.

Bam! The muted report of a gunshot in the lounge shook Grant out of his thoughts.

Damien feared the worst when they heard the gunshot that killed Judd. He gasped and cried, "Katarina!" But he quickly jumped to action. He and Grant swung the spike sides of their fire axes into the windows at the same time. They sprang up and jumped through breaking glass even while the shards were still falling, with Lou and Dylan on their heels.

Pandemonium reigned in the cocktail lounge. The rescuers lost sight of the gunmen in the rush of passengers. Those who were able to flee streamed past the delicatessen into the forward passenger compartment or out onto the promenade, leaving the stunned, the wounded, and the dead strewn among the tumbled tables and chairs like the detritus of a calamitous train wreck. Grant's breathing paused when he saw Tony's lifeless body in a wide pool of blood. He tried to yell to stop some passengers on the promenade from leaping over the rail, but his words came too late. Three passengers dove over the railing and fell into the water, so he threw a life ring over the side and stepped over Tony's body to get to the growler phone behind the bar. He nearly stumbled over another body, this one a grotesque, partially headless corpse with a giant belly and a shooter's vest. He selected the engine room and cranked the call lever until Bo answered.

"Bo, stop the boat!" Grant said. He barely found the breath to speak. "Stop the boat! People are jumping overboard." Only then did he realize that the grotesque lump of humanity under his feet was Judd. "We can't even launch the life rafts," he said to Bo. "A sniper is keeping us off the sundeck. You've got to stop the boat."

12

DEAD SHIP

The Engine Room

The call light was flashing and the sound-powered phone at the control console was growling furiously when Bo picked up the handset and spoke to Grant in the bar lounge. "Hell's bells!" he said, when he threw the handset down and turned to Todd. "People are jumping into the water. I'm shutting the engines down!"

"Wait," Todd said. "I can do a Williamson Turn, and take us right back to the spot."

"You can do that?" Bo said, with his hand ready to cut the throttles.

"Watch this," Todd said. He held the toggle over to put the rudder hard right and they felt the deck shift under their feet as the *Nighthawk* leaned into a high-speed turn. Cavitation caused the propellers to lose some of their grip on the water, shaking violently and changing their tune. Tools rattled and shifted in the workbench drawers. Todd counted the degrees of course change as indicated on the gyrocompass repeater until the boat had turned sixty degrees—then he reversed the toggle and held it to the other side to shift the rudder hard left, sending the stern sliding around in a maneuver that would make the kids drifting the rear wheels of souped-up cars in parking lots envious. When the gyrocompass showed the ship's heading was close to the reciprocal of the course he had been steering before, Todd put the rudder amidships, and said, "Okay. Bo. Shut 'em down."

"Beautiful," Bo said as he pulled the throttles back and jumped to each engine to release the compressions. The engine room was relatively quiet when the main diesel engines were silenced, with only generators and ventilators running. "Where did you learn that trick, Sprout?"

"It's in here," Todd said, holding up the *Eldridge's* book that Dana had given him.

"You did good, Sprout," Bo said, sitting on a toolbox and wiping his brow. "Yes, sir, you did really good."

"I hope they're getting life rings and the rafts over the side," Todd said. "I should go up and help."

"No," Bo said. "That will not work, Sprout. Grant said there are men shooting on the sundeck. The crew can't even get up there—those stairs are a deathtrap."

"We've got to do something, Bo. Hypothermia is going to get those people real soon. They'll freeze to death in the water this time of the year."

"Well, I don't rightly know," Bo said. "You've already done your part getting the boat turned around."

"There's got to be a way."

"Okay," Bo said, scratching his chin. "There is another way to get to the sundeck. But it is too risky, Sprout."

"Tell me, Bo. I can do it."

"I don't know about that," Bo said. "It is possible to climb up inside the smokestack, all the way to the sundeck." He pointed to the exhaust tubes above the engines. "These exhaust pipes go up inside a square casing—that's the stack you see on the sundeck. There are steel rungs that go up inside, like a ladder. But—it is too risky, Sprout."

"Great," Todd said. "That's how I'll go up."

"Hang on a minute, Sprout. It is hot as Satan's furnaces in there right now. And even though the bad gas is supposed to stay sealed inside the exhaust pipes, some always leaks into the outer casing of the stack. That is carbon monoxide, son. It's venting off right now, but it will take half an hour before you could even think about going up there."

"Those people will be dead in twenty minutes, Bo."

Bo looked at the teenager and rubbed his chin again. "This is crazy," he said. "I'm sorry I even mentioned it."

"Well, I'm going," Todd said. He started to climb onto the engine to get to the stack.

"Okay," Bo said. "If you're so bound and determined to go up there, take this." He soaked two white rags in a little sink and eyewash station near his workbench. "Put this over your mouth and nose. It might make it easier to breathe."

"Good idea," Todd said, tying the rag on his face like an outlaw. "But what's the other rag for?"

"This one is for me," Bo said, as he tied on his own over his mouth and nose.

"What?" Todd said. "You can't climb up here. Not with that bum leg."

"Get climbing, Sprout. I'm right behind you."

"But, Bo. No offense—your leg—"

Bo was on top of the engine with Todd by then. "You want to climb? Then climb! I'm only coming to pull you out when the exhaust gas knocks you out."

"Won't it knock you out, too, Bo?"

"You're right," Bo said. "You're probably going to get us both killed." He gave an urgent smack on Todd's rear end. "Now climb!"

Todd grabbed the lowest rung inside the casing and pulled himself up. The heat hit him right away. The space was not much larger than a phone booth, with two fourteen-inch exhaust tubes from the main engines in the center, plus three smaller exhaust tubes from the generators. The tubes were wrapped with heat blankets that were held on by twists of wire, the sharp end of which cut his back when he got too close. It was dark, too dark to see the next rung when he reached up for it. There was a circle of light from above—the ventilator fan—which seemed impossibly far away.

Todd stopped climbing long enough to say, "Bo, are you okay?" He felt a hand on his ankle.

"Don't stop," Bo said. "Get to the top before the gas gets to us."

Halfway up, they were separated from the aft passenger compartment by the steel plating of the stack casing. The heat and fumes were getting to Todd. When Bo coughed and cleared his throat, Todd said, "You sure you are okay, Bo? Why don't you go back down?"

To which Bo said, "You ain't got breath to waste on talking, Sprout. Just climb."

The dim light coming down from the exhaust fan illuminated the inside of the stack as they neared the top. The atmosphere was hazy with hot gas, which mixed with his own sweat to sear Todd's eyes, but he could now see the higher rungs when he reached for them.

Twenty feet from the top, Todd came to a small door. "What is this, Bo?"

To which Bo answered, "That's the hatch to the sundeck."

Todd said, "Should I open it? What if the shooters are on the other side?"

"This gas will kill us if you don't," Bo said. "Take your pick, Sprout."

"That's not much of a choice," Todd said as he began forcing the four small dogging levers around the door to move. The access was not opened that often, so it took considerable effort to swing it out on hinges that had been painted over. Then the sudden blast of fresh air and foggy sunlight assaulted Todd's senses. He took a deep breath and nearly passed out. The realization that he had been semiconscious near the end of their climb—reaching for the rungs like an automaton— hit him with a tsunami of nausea. He was barely aware that Bo had climbed up alongside him and put his head out the opening, until the older man said, "This is not right, Sprout. It's too quiet up here—too still—this sends a chill down my spine."

Sailors would call any vessel drifting with the engines shut down a "dead ship."' The *Nighthawk* seemed to be more than that in that moment, drifting without a soul in sight, in fog so thick that they could not see the water from their perch in the stack.

"What's that?" Todd said, hearing distant sounds. "Do you hear that, Bo?"

"My hearing ain't what it used to be, Sprout. Too many years in the engine room will do that to a body. What is it you hear?"

"It's people," Todd said, sickness turning to amazement on his features—then to horror. "People are calling for help. They are drowning out there in the fog, Bo. I hear people drowning in the water out there because the sides of the boat are too high for them to climb back aboard. They're screaming for help, Bo."

"Good Lord," Bo said.

Todd was already halfway out of the hatch at that point, crawling onto the ghostly silent sundeck. "I've got to release the life rafts," Todd said.

"Stay in here, son," Bo said, holding Todd back by his ankle. "Let me go out there."

Todd was already standing on the sundeck when he said, "Don't worry, Bo. I'll be back here before you could even get out of the hatch."

The young sailor took off before Bo could arrest him, sprinting between wooden benches arranged on the top deck like church pews for sun worshippers. At the same moment in which Todd arrived at the first raft, Bo saw the galley door open. Dana was standing in the doorway fifty feet away, silently waving her arms. Frantically gesturing, *No! Stop! Go back! Go back!*

The rafts, in large fiberglass canisters, were held in an inclined rack by two vertical pipes at the edge of the deck. Todd reached over the canister to pull away the two pipes and tossed them overboard. He was crouched down to release the retaining strap when Bo saw the figure with the rifle stand up on the roof of the galley, above where Dana was waving Todd off. Todd took the final step to release the raft—unclasping the pelican hook on the strap that held the raft to the rack—in the same moment in which the report of a high-power rifle cracked through the silence. The raft rolled overboard. Todd turned his head, startled by the shot, which missed him. He stood up, obviously confused, and he saw the shooter above the galley raise his weapon again.

The rifle cracked a second time. Todd was already diving behind one of the wooden benches. Splinters flew. The boy was moving as fast and as low as he could behind the benches. Bo reached toward him from inside the stack, and he yelled, "Get in here!" There was another loud crack and splinters flew again.

Todd went past the stack to the other side of the sundeck and began to release a second raft. Bo saw Justin in the door to the galley. The cook tossed an empty pot onto the roof of the galley with a hook shot from inside the doorway, startling the shooter. It was the bad guy's turn to look confused—he apparently had not expected that Justin and Dana would dare to open the door of the galley beneath his feet and out of his line of sight.

Todd released the second raft. He watched it roll off the rack while Bo saw the shooter kick the pot away. Then the man twisted the sling to his rifle around his left arm, sharpshooter fashion. Todd was moving back to the stack, staying low behind the benches. The shooter judged the boy's progress and fired three shots into the seat-back of the seats. Todd fell to the deck at the end of the bench. His left arm was partially detached, useless. He tried to crawl to the door with his legs and one arm.

Bo started out of the stack to pull Todd to safety. The boy was looking directly at the older man. The gauze bandage on his head made him look like a little drummer boy. Disbelief on his face. Shock in his eyes, his now-useless arm dragging him down, ten feet away. Bo was half out of the door in the stack when the rifle cracked again. Todd's whole body jumped from the impact in his chest. The old man could only watch in horror as the sniper fired two more rounds into the lad's lifeless body.

Bo was horrified at the blood. He pulled back into the stack by himself just as the shooter got him in his sights and narrowly missed. He pulled back into the stack when the bullet grazed the steel above his head. From inside the stack Bo could still see Todd's face. Ashen white. The blood and life gone from the boy's features, taking the spark of life from his once-bright eyes.

Bo saw Justin's arm pull Dana back into the shadows of the galley after all hope was lost. The galley door closed as Bo started back down the ladder rungs to the engine room, not sure of where he would go from there.

The Galley

Dana was a frozen statue when Justin pulled her into the galley. Catatonic. He set her aside like a salesclerk rearranging a mannequin in a display before he slammed the door and made sure it was locked. When he turned around, her gaze was lowered with a blank expression on her face. "Get yourself together," he said. He pushed her toward the mess table. "Better get under the table. We've got to take cover."

"No," she said.

Justin tried to push her under the table. "Don't freak out on me, girl," he said. "It's too late for Todd. That guy knows we are in here now. He's going to come after us."

"No," Dana said. Her voice was nearly a whisper.

"What the hell is that?" Justin said. "All you say is 'no'? Look, what he did to Todd was awful. Horrible. Nobody wanted to see that. Are you just gonna let him come through that door and murder us, too?"

"No," she said. Her voice was still barely audible. "I'm going to cut that bastard's balls off."

"Sweet Jesus!" Justin said. "I'd like to help you drive a stake in his heart. But he's got the damn gun."

"No. Here's what we're going to do," Dana said. She was perfectly composed. "You're going to unlock the door to the sundeck and get behind the washer and dryer. Show yourself when he comes in, then duck and cover." She went to the large stainless-steel refrigerator—an industrial two-door unit—and put some cereal boxes on top of it. "I'm going to get up here and I'm going to pounce on his head. I will cut his throat from ear to ear. Then I'm going to cut his fucking balls off."

They faced each other in silence for a few long seconds before Justin said, "Well, that just dills my pickle, Dana. You're going to use me as bait?"

"Fine," Dana said. She turned toward the door to the sundeck. "I'll go out there by myself and get him. You can lock the door after I'm outside."

"Wait," Justin said. He went to the one-way window over his food prep area. "Cool down, Dana. Let me think about this." He saw that the shooter had come down from the roof over their heads and that he had gone to the door in the stack, which was still open. Bo was long gone but he fired several shots blindly into the void within the stack. He stood over Todd's body with his weapon raised in one hand, his other hand in a fist, held up in a gesture of victory. Then he moved toward the galley, sweeping his rifle in search of other targets as he walked. "Here he comes," Justin said. He turned to Dana. "Yeah, we've got to do something, or this guy is going to kill us all."

"Give me a boost up," Dana said. Justin made a step with interlocked fingers. The sheath knife in the small of her back was in his face when she stepped up. He had never been close to her legs before. They were so smooth that he nearly passed out as she pulled herself up.

"Now toss some more cereal boxes up here," she said.

"Here you go," Justin said. "That's a good blind you made for yourself. You sure you never went duck hunting?"

She said, "Good luck, Justin."

He reached up and touched her hand. "It's all on you, girl. I always knew you were something special."

He unlocked the door and reached the washer and dryer in two quick strides. His heart nearly failed when Dana shifted in her lair and a box of Cheerios fell to the galley deck. A moment later the one-way window at his prep area exploded. The bullet came through and hit the coffee machine, which also burst apart as the glass carafes disintegrated. The shooter poked the muzzle of his weapon through the now-empty window frame. His masked head came into the galley a moment later. He looked around and stopped when he got to Justin. If he got in that way, he'd be on the wrong side of the galley for Dana to jump him from behind.

Damnit, Justin thought. He ducked behind the washer and dryer. *This plan is falling apart at the git-go.*

The shooter tried to climb through the window, but his full-body armor made that impossible. He withdrew from the window. Seconds later three shots hit the door to the sundeck. The bullets lost energy when they penetrated the door's stainless-steel back-plate, but they still showered Justin with fragments of hollow point ammunition ricocheting off the bulkhead behind the laundry machines. Justin choked down the urge to yell, *the door isn't locked, you dumb-duck!*

Justin heard the latch handle move and then the door opened wide. The shooter did not move. He stood motionless in the door, a backlit silhouette. *He knows we are unarmed,* Justin thought. *Standing there like a damn fool. I could take him out with my .22 squirrel gun right now, right between those beady eyes.*

Justin ducked and tried to make himself small. Three bullets came through the washer and dryer like they were cardboard boxes. *I am dead,* Justin thought. *Good night, Mother.* The killer faced the stainless cooler when he was inside the galley without suspecting that Dana was concealed behind the cereal boxes on top, then turned to approach Justin behind the white laundry machines.

The shower of cereal boxes startled the shooter. The screaming red-haired banshee woman that descended upon him in the rain of boxes was his worst nightmare. The demon landed on his back. He tried to spin her off, but she did not go down. It screamed in his ear. A shrill, terrifying sound. The she-devil's knife found his neck around the collar of his body armor. He screamed, too, but in terror. Justin joined the chorus when he jumped up with a rebel yell, "Yee-ha!"

The shooter tried to aim up at Dana. She held on to his back and plunged her knife again. He held the trigger of his assault rifle down and emptied the magazine into the ceiling tiles on full-automatic. Chunks of hung white ceiling rained down. Justin finished his rebel yell as he tackled the killer and all three of them landed in a heap on the floor of his galley. Dana rolled away and her attacker—who was now more her victim—landed hard on his back. She was on top of him while Justin beat his head with a rolling pin. The shooter was gurgling through the violent tracheotomy she had performed on him with her knife. She stood straddled above him. Saw his blood spurting. His eyes met hers with terror, awe, and resignation.

He was still conscious when Dana pulled at the body armor below his belt. She cut the straps and exposed his belt buckle. "The last thing you will ever know is me cutting your balls off," she screeched. "You're going to hell without your nuts!"

13

DARKER ANGELS

The Engine Room

B o was weary and downhearted when he came down the rungs in the stack casing. "Why, Lord?" he said. "Why did you have to take that boy?" He thought of all the shipmates he had lost over the years. Taylor washed overboard in a typhoon. Benson and Evans in a boiler room flash fire. Napier, when his appendix burst in the South Atlantic, far from any hospital. Plus, all who had passed ashore, from car accidents and disease and the malice of others. Then again, he could never forget what Bull Dolan and the good old boys had done to his brother. "Why not me?" Bo said as he descended. *Why am I still here? Living in a body that has been broken and abused. Carrying on with the pain in my joints and this sorrow in my heart?*

"Why that boy?" Bo said, when he reached the bottom rung. "That wasn't right."

With Ike and Tina shut down and only the generators running, his domain was eerily quiet when he dropped down to the deck plates— and came face-to-face with a long-haired bearded giant in bib coveralls, training an assault rifle point-blank into his face.

"Let's get going," the giant said. "Make the boat go, right now."

Bo was numb. For a few seconds he looked at the giant, face-to-face with one of *them* for the first time. "You heard me, darkie," the man said. "Start these engines, right now."

"I don't rightly know that I can do that," Bo said. He slowly withdrew the white rag from the back pocket of his coveralls and wiped the sweat from his face and neck. "You can't just turn the key on these motors. There's a procedure to follow."

"I know the goddamn procedure," Behr said. "I worked on a Mississippi towboat once. I'll get these diesels running all by myself. But you know this layout so you're going to do it."

"Fact is, I'm a tired old man," Bo said. "And you caught me at a time when I do not rightly care if I live to see another long, hard day. Do what you want to do."

"You old fool," Behr said. "A lot of people are going to die if this boat isn't moving in five minutes. That will be on you."

"How did you get in here, anyway?" Bo said. He was regaining his senses, coming out of the funk of the stack-gases and the sight of Todd's assassination. Maybe there was a way to stop this giant's murder spree.

"I told you I worked on the river," Behr said. "There's always an escape hatch from the engine room. All I had to do was find a manhole cover on the freight deck."

"Oh, I knew that," Bo said. "I knew you came in the back way." He put the white rag in his pocket and withdrew the red rag. He had a plan when he wiped the controls as he set them to start the engines. "What I meant was, how did you get your fat ass through that little scuttle?"

Bo started Tina before Behr could respond. The piercing sound of the air-starts was followed by a slow, steady rumbling as Tina came to life, followed by Ike. Then Bo pointed at the control panel in front of the engines. "Okay, big man," Bo said. "Now you can make us go."

"You must think I'm stupid," Behr said. He pushed the mushroom-shaped button to send control to the wheelhouse. Then the transfer bell was ringing, signifying that the wheelhouse could take control. "Surprise, you old fool. I learned our man in the wheelhouse how to take control up there."

The engines came up to full power. The attackers had regained control of the *Nighthawk*.

"I'm done with you, darkie," Behr said as soon as the boat started moving. "Now it's time for you to die."

When Behr turned around, Bo was gone.

The Galley

Dana sat on the deck and put her head in her hands, barely breathing, gazing down, as if waking from a dream in a deep sleep. She focused on some scattered corn flakes and Cheerios on the usually spotless deck of Justin's galley. *How did that cereal get there?* The shooter was also a mystery, lying on his back in front of her, taking his final gurgling breaths through the violent tracheotomy gash that someone had knifed into his neck. His eyelids were half closed. The eyes had stopped moving and his vacuous gaze had turned up toward his battered brow. Blood was everywhere. When his chest stopped heaving and the horrible death rattle ended, she realized that her own lungs were starving for air.

"Dana," Justin said, "breathe."

With Justin's urging she gulped a mighty breath of air and exhaled forcefully. Then another. And another deep breath. She was exhausted. Completely spent, as if she had crossed the finish line of some dream-state marathon that had been run in another reality. As if she had left it all on that bizarre racecourse in a separate dimension. When she heard the engines starting and the deck under her buttocks began to vibrate again, she knew that the previous few seconds of her life— which seemed like an eternity—had not been a dream. The race was real, and it was not over. It had just begun, and she gulped deep breaths, trying to regain the pace. Reality was there, barely out of reach, slightly out of sync with her thoughts. She struggled to reunite with the inexorable flow of time, moment to moment.

"Dana, are you okay?" Justin said. "Are you hurt?" He was kneeling over the shooter's body, unfastening the assault rifle from the combat-sling that attached it to his chest.

"I'm okay," she said between gulps of air. Even as she secretly thought, *so this is what crazy feels like. Did that really happen? Did I do that?* Her head remained bowed when she said, "How about you, Justin?"

"We're alive," Justin said. He took a magazine full of ammunition from the shooter's body and put it into the rifle. "You were scary, Dana.

I never saw anything like that. You were a fearsome thing, but you saved us." He checked the operation of the weapon and pointed it out the door to the sundeck. "This scope is all screwed up. The lenses are cracked and screwed up inside. No wonder he couldn't hit shit."

It took all her energy to raise her head and look at him. He was moving on, resuming the race as if nothing had just happened. As if the two of them had not just killed a man. The deck began to vibrate more forcefully as the engines came up to full power and the boat began to move through the water. The sickening rolling of an inept helmsman resumed, rocking her world from side to side. Through the open door to the sundeck she could see the fog-bound water gyrating like a tilt-a-whirl carnival ride. She met Justin's eyes. He said, "You sure you're not hurt?"

She nodded and said, "I'm okay."

"You don't look okay," he said. She had never noticed how brown and kind his eyes were. "You sit right there," Justin said. "Somebody's got to do something about the asshole that hijacked our boat." He stood up and faced the wheelhouse, which was at the far end of a hallway lined with the crew's staterooms. "I guess that's me."

No, she thought. He could not be capable of slipping back into insanity and killing again. How could he not be revolted at the thought of taking another human life? Not the affable big man with his Southern charm—his quirky sense of humor—and his silly little sayings: "happy as a tick on a hound dog" and "if the creek don't rise." Justin was no murderer. The world had truly gone crazy.

Oh my God, she thought, coming out of her own personal fugue state. Remembering the insanity that had overcome her when she descended on the shooter. *They have turned us all into monsters.*

She started to pick up her sheath knife, which was between her and the shooter's lifeless torso, covered in blood. But she could not touch it. She stood up and faced Justin. He was getting ready to use the assault rifle that he had taken from the sniper. There were no words. "Just sit down, Dana," he said. "You've done enough."

Her mouth moved but no words came. She turned away from him and bolted out the door to the sundeck. She ran outside and gasped when she saw Todd's lifeless remains, forty feet away. It still felt like the dream was continuing when she reached the rescue boat on the starboard side and her hand pushed the button to energize the hydraulics. She kicked the pelican hook to release the bridle that held the inflatable boat in the cradle and pushed the lever to swing it over the side. Suspended from the davit by a single cable, the small boat began to swing from side to side in reaction to the vessel's rolling. A crazy, un-syncopated pendulum fifty feet above the water.

Dana froze when she looked down. The water was far below, and the little boat was a moving target in front of her. In her mind she was back on the sailing vessel *Calliope* in that moment, losing her grip on the topsail yard, falling—

Her leap into the small boat happened in a trance. She pulled the self-lowering toggle hanging alongside the cable and the clutch to the winch released, allowing the boat to freefall. The boat's rubber pontoons banged and bounced off the side of the *Nighthawk* and then swung out as the vessel took another crazy roll. She stood in the boat and pulled the toggle harder and the boat fell faster. It banged against the side of the speeding ferry again at the promenade deck and continued to descend. She was startled when passengers rose from their hiding spots behind the bulwarks and screamed, "Wait. Don't leave us! Take us! You can't leave us!"

She ignored the passengers' pleading and pulled the descent toggle with all her might.

The rigid-hull inflatable boat hit the rushing water alongside the big boat's hull hard. She strained to release the hook that set the craft and its lone occupant free in an exploding torrent of water, and the *Nighthawk*—now a ship of horrors—swiftly pulled away and disappeared into the fog.

The Generator Room

The main propulsion engines were roaring to life and Behr's back was turned when Bo slipped into the generator room. He felt the deck plates under his feet heave and tilt as the boat resumed its wild, rolling motion after control was transferred back to the attacker in the wheelhouse. He knew that he did not have much time before the giant redneck would come looking for him with murder in his eyes. And he knew what he had to do.

The old engineer went straight to the main electrical panel and snapped the rows of circuit breakers that would extinguish the lighting in all the machinery spaces. Each click plunged a section of his domain into darkness. The emergency lights came on a few moments later, but they left large swaths of the spaces in shadows, where Bo knew every inch.

He smashed the glass to set off the carbon-dioxide deluge system in the generator room. The squealing siren sounded immediately when the fire-suppression system was activated, signaling fifteen seconds before the carbon-dioxide gas would issue from the red nozzles overhead. The automatic watertight door was linked to the fire-suppression system, so its own warning sounded at the same time. Fifteen seconds to evacuate. If the giant was crafty or was afraid to come into the generator room, Bo could go up the emergency scuttle and be on the freight deck before the gas overcame him. Or maybe the giant's own hate and arrogance would be his undoing.

Bo went into the half-light behind the banks of diesel generators and felt his way to the starboard side, where he knew two deck plates deeper in the shadows were not bolted down. He always left these plates loose so he could get to the raw seawater valves in the bilge.

Bo quickly tossed those deck plates aside and stepped around the two-foot drop into the bilges their absence had created. He got behind the main electrical panel with a monkey wrench—and he waited.

Water vapor condensed around the freezing carbon-dioxide gas when it began gushing down from the nozzles above the generators. He did not see Behr come through the opening of the watertight door, which had started to creep closed. That was okay. He did not have to see things directly in his shadowy domain. The emergency spotlight over the door cast the giant's shadow into the generator room as he passed through. Bo forced Todd and the others out of his thoughts.

He was tired and he was old. He did not have to win for himself, but there were many lives at stake. This giant full of hate had to be stopped.

Bo stayed behind the main panel and tossed the wrench to the starboard side, past the missing deck plates. Behr said, "Goddamn it!" when he put one foot into the hole and stumbled.

Bo jumped from behind the main electrical panel. He reached the watertight door when it was halfway closed and went through into the engine room. *God steady me,* he thought. These were the moments that counted. His hand found a tin can under a leaky valve in an oil reservoir and he tossed the lubricating fluid onto the deck plates on the other side of the closing door, moments before Behr's imposing form came into the glow of the emergency lights.

Behr raised his rifle and said, "I'm going to kill you, nigg—" But the giant's feet found the oil slick on the deck plates. His boots went out from under his top-heavy bulk and he fell headfirst into the door, which closed around his hips. He twisted sideways, trying to get free, but it was too late. The knife-edge of the door squeezed tighter.

Bo reached the switch to stop the door before it cut the giant in half. The gears ground to a halt as Behr screamed, "Get me out of here!"

Bo still had his hand on the switch when he said, "You didn't have one of these automatic doors on your little towboat, did you?"

Behr screamed vile obscenities at Bo and repeated, "I'm going to kill you!" As if he was mentally incapable of accepting that he was no longer large and in charge. As if nothing in his life had prepared him to face the reality that this skinny, limping old black man had thoroughly outsmarted him.

"I don't think I'm going to let you kill anyone else today," Bo said. "The question is, do I let you live? What is a God-fearing man to do?"

Behr pushed and scratched at the door while he said, "Let me out of here!"

"I hear you," Bo said. "But what should I do now? What is the proper thing, I ask myself? Do I twist my wrist left and open his door—or do I go right and close it all the way? Either way, I can walk away and let the gas kill you. You know about carbon-dioxide gas, don't you? It's odorless and invisible and heavier than air, you know. It's filling up the generator room now, and soon it will spill through the opening in that door and displace the oxygen where you are, and you will inhale but there won't be a bit of oxygen in your breaths and you will simply pass out and die. I ask you, what should a God-fearing man do?"

"No!" Behr said. He was almost pleading. Almost a broken beast. "Let me get out of here."

"The question is," Bo said, "are you a man, or a monster?"

"Goddamn you, open the door!" Behr said. "A God-fearing man can't kill me! You can't do it. Open this door."

"You may be right," Bo said. "Truth be known—there's nobody alive who knows this—I did set out to kill a man once. God help me, I did. The man who lynched my brother had to die. That is how I saw it as a young lad of fifteen years, anyway. I set out to kill Big Bull Dolan with his own gun. Man alive, those good old boys were so arrogant. They would come across the railroad tracks for some brown sugar in the afternoon. One day I snatched Big Bull's shotgun from the window rack in his pickup truck and stuck it in his face when he came out of Hattie-Mae's shack, buckling his pants up. I tell you, the good old boys were untouchable. They knew no black man would dare take a white man's gun and turn it back on him. Big Bull did not even go for the thirty-eight revolver in his back pocket. No, he just laughed at me and pulled a fifth of whiskey out of his other pocket. 'Git out of here, boy,' Big Bull said, taking a swig. 'You're just going to cause a whole lot of trouble down here.'

"Thing is, I knew he was right," Bo said. "If I shot him, those good old boys would have lynched a dozen black men and burned every house on our side of the tracks to the ground—they weren't nothing more than shacks, anyway. So I dropped his shotgun without pulling the trigger and I went to Memphis to live with my aunt. I lived in fear for years, thinking that the police would come knocking on my door just for threatening Big Bull. Worse than that, I still wake up in a sweat sometimes thinking I did pull the trigger."

"Shut up!" Behr said. "Shut your mouth and open this door."

"Big man, you don't listen very well," Bo said. "I've been telling you why I won't close this door all the way—why I won't cut you clean in half."

"You can't do that," Behr said. "Let me out of here, or everybody is going to die."

"That may be," Bo said. "Let me tell you, your hate and your threats aren't keeping you alive. I have seen your kind do a terrible thing today. I have seen the life of a fine young man cut short by your hate. A lot of people might rejoice if you die, right now. But I will not finish it— I will not kill you, because that will put out the light in my own soul. You got yourself stuck there by your own evil deeds. I had to stop you, and there you are."

"You listen to me, you stupid old coon," Behr said. "We're all going to die if I don't get out of here."

The Wheelhouse

Justin stood at the rail on the sundeck and watched Dana start the outboard motor on the small boat and disappear into the fog. For a few seconds he looked into the empty water where he had last seen her. Her departure left him oddly unsettled. He felt some sort of urgent bond with her after they combined forces to defeat a mortal attacker—this was a strange new feeling—and he wondered what it was and whether she felt it too. He looked up and saw dark gray exhaust smoke spewing out of the stack and coalescing into a smudge of greasy brown fog hanging low in the sky behind the boat. Todd's body was there near the base of the smokestack, only thirty feet away. He had never seen the water rush by the side of the *Nighthawk* as fast as it was at that moment.

The big boat had to be stopped.

He examined the assault rifle in his hands and made sure he understood how to operate it. He pulled the bolt back far enough to be sure there was a round in the chamber and checked that the safety was off. The scope was broken, but that would not matter inside the wheelhouse.

Justin went into the galley and stepped around the shooter's body. He opened the door to the long narrow passageway that led to the wheelhouse. Some outside light was coming in through the portholes in the crew's staterooms, where the doors were open and held back by retaining hooks to keep them from banging around when the boat was under way. The boat was rolling heavily. His shoulders bounced off the bulkheads a few times as he inched forward. Loose articles were rolling around in the drawers and lockers in the staterooms. Saint's can of shaving cream and Lou's sea boots. Another of Dylan's books. Todd's music player and headset slid off his bunk and fell to the deck.

He took a deep breath and held the rifle in one hand while he tapped the code to unlock the deadbolt in the door to the wheelhouse. He thought about Dana and pushed the heavy door wide open with a rebel yell, "Yee-ha!"

The windshield ahead of the helm was shattered, allowing cold mist to flow into the wheelhouse to coat the interior with moisture. The man at the helm was just a skinny kid with tattoos and unkempt hair who turned and looked at him with droopy eyelids. He could barely stand up, with a posture that was more of an S-curve than a steady stance. He was obviously stoned to the point of semiconsciousness, with his jaw hanging, begging to be hit—which Justin obliged with the butt of the rifle, reducing the "helmsman" to a heap on the deck.

Justin reached over the tattooed kid to pull the throttle levers to neutral, and the *Nighthawk* coasted to a stop.

One sweep of the wheelhouse assured him that there were no attackers in the shadows. The sight of Tom Chapman lying on the deck burned his eyes like a laser and he turned away. *Oh, Tommy—why?* It was unthinkable that the captain was gone. Justin had stood so many watches with Tom in this very wheelhouse. He sometimes sailed as an able-bodied seaman when the crew was short, and he often took the helm on the last trip back to Hyannis at night so the deckhands could clean the boat. Now Tommy's spotlessly clean and well-organized wheelhouse was battered and damp, and Tommy was gone. The keystone of all that was right and good about the *Nighthawk* was in shambles. It was unimaginable.

He grabbed the microphone and called the Coast Guard on the VHF radio. "Coast Guard, this is the *Nighthawk*," Justin said. "We've been attacked. They are shooting people and the captain is dead. We need help now!" He looked at the electronic chart display. "We're over here by Halfmoon Shoal. Our position is forty-one degrees and twenty-eight minutes north, seventy degrees and ten minutes west. Come back."

When the Coast Guard asked Justin for the exact number of persons onboard, he said, "How the hell do I know that? Hundreds! This is the damn Nantucket ferry for Christ sakes! Just get out here!"

"Captain," the Coast Guard said, "anchor your vessel at this time and have all persons onboard put on life jackets."

"I'm not the captain," Justin said, annoyed by the standard bureaucratic response. "I'm the cook. I told you, the captain has been shot and there are people who jumped overboard all around in the water. They're killing us, don't you get it?"

Another voice came on the radio and broke into the conversation. "Break, break," the voice said. "*Nighthawk*, this is the Coast Guard Cutter *Hammerhead*. We are en route to your position. We'll be alongside you in sixteen minutes—hang in there!"

"Thank God," Justin said. Then he threw down the microphone and grabbed the unconscious attacker by the scruff. He slung the assault rifles over his shoulder and dragged him out of the pilothouse, dropping him to the deck like a sack of potatoes in the hallway long enough to take the portable radio from Grant's stateroom. Then he continued to the galley, where he dropped the kid again. He looked at Dana's sheath knife on the deck near the sniper. It had a short blade that was razor sharp and Justin did not know why he picked it up. It occurred to him that he was tampering with evidence in some sort of big-deal investigation that was bound to happen, but he did not give a shit. He took the knife and went out onto the sundeck with the stoned kid in tow and two assault rifles slung over his shoulder.

He tossed the knife overboard where it would fall to the bottom of Nantucket Sound, never again to see the light of day.

He saw Todd's lifeless form again as he stood the semiconscious attacker up at the top of the stirs to the promenade. He wondered where Dana was and hoped that she was okay and that she might find her way back to the *Nighthawk* now that he had stopped the vessel. Only then, standing at the top of the stairway to whatever scene from Hell was unfolding on the passenger deck, did he notice that he knew this kid he was dragging. He couldn't recall the name, but he knew that this nitwit had worked in the snack bar for a brief time, and that he had proven himself to be a first-rate asshole.

"Yee-ha!" Justin yelled. He pushed the kid down to land hard on the promenade at the foot of the stairs.

The Hammerhead

Jack had just signed his retirement letter when Neal called down the ladder from the pilothouse.

"Get up here, Skipper," Neal said. "Something serious is happening on the island ferry."

Jack got to the pilothouse in time to overhear the middle of Justin's call to the OPCEN for help. "Plot a course to Halfmoon Shoal," he said to Spokes. "Call the engine room and get the chief engineer up here. I want him to lead the boarding team."

When he couldn't stand it any longer, he broke into the OPCEN's transmissions. "*Nighthawk*, this is the Coast Guard Cutter *Hammerhead*," he said. "We're en route to your position. We'll be alongside you in sixteen minutes—hang in there!"

After the *Nighthawk* came back with "Thank God," Jack turned to Neal, and he said, "What the hell is going on here? Didn't the OPCEN talk to the *Nighthawk* when this shitshow started?"

"Aye, Master Chief," Neal said. "They came back after you went below and said they were headed back to Hyannis with trouble onboard."

"And you didn't think that was important enough to call me?"

"Gee, Master Chief, don't blow a gasket. The ferry asked for the police to meet them in Hyannis and the OPCEN didn't think the trouble was all that serious."

"Damnit, Neal. These professional mariners are not like weekend yacht-types. They don't cry 'Mayday' every time somebody has a hangnail.

When they say trouble, they mean serious shit!"

Chief Mike Barlow came up from the engine room, wiping his hands with a rag. "What's the deal?" he said. He was a lanky man with thinning hair like dry straw and tattoos on his wrists.

"It's a shitty deal, Mike," Jack said. "This is no drill. There is a full-blown terror attack on the *Nighthawk* over by Halfmoon Shoal—people shot and people in the water—the whole show sucks. I am going to have to send you into a hornet's nest. Pick whoever you want for your boarding party and gear up for action. Neal is going to take the small boat and round up survivors in the water."

"No sweat," Chief Mike said. "We're on it, Jack."

14

CHANGING TIDES

The Passenger Deck

Matthias and Colt—with Katarina in tow—had rushed through the passenger deck to the aft compartment amid a flood tide of passengers fleeing from the cocktail lounge. When they reached the rear booths of the pet area, they turned around and fired at their pursuers, without regard for innocent lives. A few passengers ran away from the crossfire, out to the promenade—the college boy in the Roger Williams sweatshirt was one of them—and decided to take their chances in the water. They jumped over the rail before Grant could stop them. Lou took cover behind a trash bin and fired a few shots over Matthias's head, but the rest of the crew were effectively pinned down in the hallway between the forward and aft compartments, near the game room and the passenger restrooms.

Sean leaned out of the game room and motioned for Grant, Damien, and Dylan to join him in the relative safety of the video arcade. "What happened to him?" Grant said when he saw one of the attackers slumped in the corner. His face was a bloody mess and his torso was tied up with the power cord from a video game.

"That's Stumpy," Sean said. He pointed to the assault rifle on the deck. "He doesn't talk much, but he brought us that AK-47. Help yourself."

"I'll take that," Damien said. He dropped his fire axe and picked up the weapon. "Do we have spare ammo?"

"Check Stump's pack," Sean said. "They came by here too fast, in the middle of a crowd of hostages. I could not get a clear shot at the bad guys. Sorry to say, it looks like they duct-taped that shotgun around Katarina's neck to the kid's wrist—the one the leader called 'Colt.'"

They were startled to hear a rebel yell from somewhere outside, "Yee-ha!"

"What the hell was that?" Sean said.

"That sounds like Justin," Dylan said. "Cover me, Lou. I'll go check it out." He sprinted to the forward compartment in time to see a skinny man land in a heap at the bottom of the stairs from the sundeck. Justin came down to the promenade a second later, with one assault rifle in his hands and another slung across his back. He followed Dylan to the game room, dragging his prisoner by the scruff. The other crew-members were shocked to see broad swaths of the sniper's blood on his tee shirt and pants.

"Damn, Justin," Grant said, when Justin dropped tossed his prisoner on the deck in the game room. "Where did you get this one?"

"This piece of shit was in the wheelhouse," Justin said. "I think he's the one who shot Tommy. Unless someone can prove otherwise."

"That's Zack," Damien said. "I came over to the boat with my father the day he fired him. If I'd only known—"

"Don't blame yourself," Grant said. "We all knew he was a creep, but Roland believes that everybody deserves a chance at a job. None of us guessed that he worked here just long enough to probe our security. Let's tie him up with Stumpy"

"I'll take one of those rifles," Dylan said. Justin kept the rifle with the broken scope that he had taken from the sniper and handed Zack's AK-47 to Dylan, who said, "Is this the gun that—?"

"Yup, that's the gun that got Tommy," Justin said. "I almost threw it overboard."

"Hate the shooter, not the gun," Lou said. "Turning their own weapons back on these jerks feels just right to me."

Damien and Dylan wrapped another power cord around Zack while Justin told them how Dana trapped and ambushed the sniper in the galley after he shot Todd. There was stunned silence when he was done with his account of her ferocity after Todd's murder. Until Justin said, "You know I am not sure, but I might have killed the sniper. Maybe I stuck a kitchen knife in his throat after she got him down. It all happened so fast."

Sean guessed that Justin was trying to cover for Dana. "Talk to a lawyer before you make any statement," he said. "That goes for all of us. I say it to piece-of-shit perps every day, but it goes for the good guys too."

"First we got to live through this," Lou said. "I'd rather be judged by twelve men than carried by six."

Grant said, "Justin, where is Dana now?"

"She's gone," Justin said. "She launched herself over the side in the rescue boat."

"We'll worry about that later," Grant said. "Right now, I have to get to the wheelhouse and call the Coast Guard."

"You don't have to go up there," Justin said. "I called them five minutes ago. A patrol boat came back and said they would be here right quick." Justin took the mate's portable radio from his back pocket and handed it to Grant. "I brought this so you can talk to them when they get closer."

"That's strong work, Justin," Grant said. He took the portable radio and tuned it to channel 16, the calling and distress frequency. "The question is, what do we do in the meantime? We have these bastards outgunned right now."

"Let's talk to them," Damien said.

"You could do that," Sean said. "First, you might want to make a show of force. Just two shots from each of these weapons—over everybody's heads and all at once—would demonstrate that we have superior firepower."

"That would get their attention," Grant said. "Then who would do the talking?"

"That's me," Damien said. "I'll talk."

"That will work," Sean said. "Aim high because there are people hiding in booths and under tables. Just don't get into a firefight right now. Everybody must play it cool. If they return fire after we send a few rounds their way, just take cover and let them expend their ammo. If they get excited and desperate, they might decide to go out in a blaze of glory. That wouldn't be good for their hostage."

"All right," Grant said. "That's how we'll play it. Are we all ready?"

"Just give the word," Lou said, from across the hall.

"Okay," Grant said. "Now!"

The volley from their captured weapons sent a hail of lead into the aft cabin and left all their ears momentarily deafened and ringing. But they clearly heard the passengers hiding in booths and under tables cry. "Stop it!" the passengers said. "Stop shooting! Please!"

"Everybody, stay low," Damien said, loud enough to be heard throughout the space. "Matthias and Colt, listen up. We know who you are. Most of your friends are in no position to help to you now. You are outnumbered and outgunned. Let's talk."

There was only silence from the attackers, broken by the sobbing and pleading of passengers.

"Matthias, the Coast Guard will be here very soon," Damien said. "Why don't we settle this before they get here? Maybe we can all be better off if we make a deal now."

"You can go to hell!" Matthias said, without showing himself. "I have more friends than you can imagine, all ready to rise up and live free or die for our cause. The revolution has begun. It will sweep across this country like a wildfire! We the people will eradicate the deep state and the blood of the bureaucrats will run in the streets. No power on Earth can stop us now."

"Keep him talking," Sean said, speaking softly.

"Tell me about it," Damien said. He had to yell loudly to be heard by the attackers. "I want to learn."

"We are everywhere," Matthias said, launching into a preachy rant. "We're in the forests and the hills and the open range, wherever a man can be free of the imperial tyranny that is dragging our great nation under." Lou circled his index finger around his temple. *He's nuts.*

"That's good," Sean said. "Make him talk about his movement, whatever it is. Ask him if he is the leader and who will take over if he falls."

"This guy is delusional," Dylan said. "Talking isn't going to change his mind."

"Of course," Sean said. "The trick is to make the other kid—Colt—realize how crazy his leader is."

"You don't think the kid hasn't heard all this before?" Damien said. Matthias was still ranting, "Blood and Soil. The new World Order. The Deep State."

"Let him think about what will happen next," Sean said.

"Matthias," Damien said out loud. "Who will take over if your fight ends here?"

Matthias had no answer for this.

The crew tensed when there was movement at the back of the passenger cabin. Katarina was made to slowly stand and show herself above the partitions around the booths. The kill-noose and shotgun remained at her neck, still taped to Colt's hand. Even more stunning was the sight of a young girl rising behind the partition, holding a Yorkie puppy.

"Damn it," Grant said. It was the girl in the plaid skirt he had spoken to before this nightmare began. That seemed like a century ago, even though barely thirty minutes had passed since Matthias seized Judd's gun. "That kid must have been hiding under the same table where those creeps took cover."

"Shit," Damien said. "This just keeps getting worse and worse."

"Don't give up," Lou said. "Maybe they're ready to deal."

"Let's find out," Grant said. He slowly stood up and stepped into the hallway. Damien joined him a few seconds later, in full view of the attackers and their hostages. Which drew a plaintive cry from Katarina. "Damien," she said. "I'm sorry."

"Shut up!" Matthias said. Then he and Colt began to inch sideways with their human shields firmly held toward the crew. Colt had the shotgun at Katarina's neck and Matthias held the girl with the crook of his arm under her jaw. The girl was crying and clutching her Yorkie as they sidestepped gradually toward the door to the promenade. The puppy was yapping and barking frantically.

The rest of the boat crew emerged from cover and followed the attackers onto the promenade. Matthias and Colt were facing them with their hostages, slowly retreating backward towards the stern, with no place to go, except the aft stairs to the freight deck. The pack of dogs that had escaped their masters was drawn to the promenade by the Yorkie's barking and they ran clear around outside the passenger deck like Greyhounds on a track. The girl in the plaid skirt tried to restrain her puppy but he reached Matthias's forearm with his teeth and began biting.

"Damn you," Matthias said when he crossed his AK-47 in front of the girl to hold her while he pulled his right arm clear of her neck. He grabbed the Yorkie and tossed it over the side. The helpless animal cried all the way down into the fog and freezing water. The girl let loose an agonizing, painful scream as her pet disappeared. Then the mismatched quartet—vicious attackers and terrified hostages together—disappeared down the stairs to the freight deck.

The Aft Passenger Cabin

Sean was primed to pursue Matthias and Colt on the promenade with the others, but he could not dismiss the plaintive cries of some passengers who had been injured in the crossfire. He returned to the passenger compartment and swept through booths and tables to locate and comfort the wounded. He found three with what appeared to be non-life-threatening injuries, and two—a young woman and an elderly man—with severe gunshot wounds. He enjoined some able-bodied passengers to help him apply direct pressure to stanch the bleeding. There was a Korean War veteran's baseball cap near where the man had fallen, and Sean used it as a compress on a gaping hole in his abdomen. He asked another passenger to take over tending to the man when he heard a voice calling, "Abbey! Abbey, where are you?"

Sean stood up and found Ezra in a crowd of shocked and panicked passengers in the hallway by the game room. He went to him and said,

"Ezra, she's okay. Abbey was not hurt. She's in the ladies' room with Helen."

"I've got to get to her," Ezra said. But Sean shook him by the shoulder and said, "Doctor, there are severely injured people over there who need your help."

Ezra blinked, as if awakening from a deep sleep. "Where?" he said. "How many?"

"We have at least two serious gunshot wounds, and lots of other injuries."

"My bag is in my car," Ezra said.

"We can't get down there now," Sean said. "These people need your brain, not your bag."

Ezra turned toward the game room and said, "What about this man?" He pointed to Stumpy. "Is that—?"

"Yup, that's the asshole who threatened Abbey," Sean said. He turned toward the aft cabin and Ezra followed. "He's alive, but he's going to have a hell of a headache. We'll get to him later."

Ezra descended on the wounded and quickly brought order to the lifesaving efforts. Nurses, firemen, and military veterans gravitated to him as he made his initial assessment of the injuries, and he assigned each volunteer to a specific task. A grown-up Eagle Scout put his jacket on a woman lying on the deck and held her mangled hand above her head to slow the bleeding while a woman with emergency medical training sat with a man who might be having a heart attack.

The sight of Justin coming back into the passenger cabin holding an AK-47 in bloodstained kitchen garb panicked some of the passengers. Dylan was with him, and he went to Sean and Ezra. He said, "Grant wants us to get all the passengers on the bow in life jackets."

"These patients cannot be moved," Ezra said. "Not until they are stabilized. Then we must get them to a trauma center as quickly as possible."

"You heard the doctor," Sean said. "Take everyone else to the bow. And give me that AK—it's time to finish this thing."

Justin handed the assault rifle to Sean. Dylan opened the utility closet near the game room to get a large first aid kit, which he handed to Ezra. Then he and Justin began moving the passengers who were ambulatory to the bow, taking life jackets from under the bench seats as they went.

Sean went to the ladies' room and told Helen to open the door. She burst out into his arms holding Olivia, and she said, "Thank God, you're okay."

"It's not over yet," Sean said. "The Coast Guard is coming soon, so take the kids to the bow with everybody else. And keep that pistol well hidden, just in case."

"You've got to stay with us now," she said.

"Don't worry," Sean said. "I'll be fine."

Abbey saw Ezra when she emerged from the ladies' room and she tried to go to him. Sean stopped her and said, "Ezra has to be a doctor right now."

Ezra saw her too, and he stood above the injured and held his palms up, *sorry*, *not now.*

Helen held Olivia in her arms and took Abbey by the hand to join the passengers heading towards the bow, with Brianna at her side holding Teddy's hand, and Ricky urging another older woman to keep up. Sean watched his family disappear into the procession and wondered if he would ever really understand what had transpired in the ladies' room.

The 'Tween Deck

"Wait!" Grant said, when he and the crewmen reached the top of the stairs to the freight deck. They watched as Matthias and Colt inched down the steps with their hostages held in front of themselves as human shields. "They'd like nothing better than for us to follow them on the stairs."

"That's how Saint bought it," Lou said. "We'd be fish in a barrel on those steps."

"Dylan, there might be injuries on the passenger deck," Grant said. "I need you and Justin to go back and help those people. Get everyone in life jackets and move them to the bow until the Coast Guard gets here."

"Okay," Dylan said as he and Justin departed. "Good luck."

"Look!" Lou said. "They didn't go all the way down to the freight deck. They ducked into that alcove to the 'tween deck."

"Why would they do that?" Damien said. "There's nothing but parked cars on the 'tween deck."

"That alcove would be the perfect place to ambush us on the stairs," Lou said. "We should double back on the other stairs and outflank their asses."

"There might not be time for that," Grant said. The others looked at him for an answer. "That kid Colt was driving the catering truck that came aboard last, with our old friend Zack riding shotgun. I think these guys want to get to that truck."

"Christ almighty," Damien said. "What are you thinking? Is there a bomb in the truck?"

At that point Sean came out of the passenger compartment and huddled with them at the top of the stairs. "A truck bomb?" Sean said. "That's how I would attack a conference. I would pack that truck full of explosives and park it at the back door to the kitchen. Anybody who lived through the explosion would be easy prey coming out the front door."

"Then we have to get all the passengers into life rafts," Grant said. "Let them set off their bomb after everybody is off the boat."

"It's not going to be that easy," Sean said. "The doctor says that some seriously wounded people in the aft cabin can't be moved."

"That's one problem," Damien said. "Plus, people are paralyzed with fear and hiding all over the boat. It won't be easy to coax them all out of cover and into life rafts."

"Jeez," Grant said. "That doesn't leave us any choice. I'll have to go down there."

"Not so fast, Captain," Sean said. He looked at Lou, who silently nodded. "Why don't you let me and Lou handle this part?"

Grant agreed, and Sean looked at Lou and said, "Fire and maneuver. Right?"

"Right," Lou said. "Let's do this."

Sean stepped onto the stairs first, holding the butt of the AK-47 Justin had presented to him in his armpit so he could aim over the barrel without using the scope. Lou stood with his weapon at his shoulder with the iron sights trained on the alcove until Sean stopped. Then Sean covered while Lou passed him on the stairs. When they reached the alcove, Sean produced his compact mirror and used it to scan around the corners.

"Clear," Sean said. Lou slipped onto the 'tween deck and took cover between two parked cars, and Sean followed. Since Dylan had secured the overhead lights, the 'tween deck was in shadows, except for a small shaft of light coming through the alcove from the stairs, and the bright light streaming through the freight deck's large open stern.

Lou said, "They must have gone to the aft end of this line of cars. That would put them right above the truck."

"Let's go," Sean said.

Matthias had other plans. He was indeed behind the last car on the 'tween deck. He held his AK-47 above his head like a Baghdad street fighter and fired several shots over the cars with his thumb on the trigger. "That's far enough!" Matthias said. "Any closer and both these bitches die."

"Okay," Sean said, loud enough to be heard by the shooter. "We can wait."

When Grant and Damien joined them on the 'tween deck, Sean urged them to stay low. The four of them were huddled behind the same car, when Sean said, "A standoff is a win for us, if it keeps them away from that truck."

Grant said, "So we just sit here and wait for the Coast Guard?"

"What else can we do?" Damien said. "Unless we can talk him into releasing his hostages. We could say we won't stop him from going to the truck if he leaves Katarina and that girl behind."

"That's worth a try," Sean said. "But there's one other thing that's bothering me—did any of you get a shot at that big beast in coveralls—the one they call Behr?"

"Not me," Lou said. Nor Damien.

"Damnit, with all this action I forgot about him," Grant said. "But I think I know where he is—and it isn't good. He must be in the engine room."

"I'd better go help Bo," Lou said. But Grant shook his head no. Grant said, "You are needed here, Lou. Let me go down there."

"Good luck," Damien said, as Grant stayed low in the shadows and slipped away on the 'tween deck.

The Engine Room

Grant went up the stairs to the promenade and made his way to the bow, where Dylan and Justin had gathered as many passengers as they were able. Some of the dogs that had been running loose on the promenade had found their masters, and humans and pets both celebrated the reunions. Butch was there as well, having led the sixty-two lucky passengers from the lower hold up to join the larger group that had endured the attack in the cocktail lounge.

"Dylan, I need you to go up to the sundeck and launch the life rafts. We're not ready to abandon ship yet, but maybe some of the people who jumped overboard will be able to get into them."

A passenger said, "Shouldn't we get into the rafts now?"

"Not yet," Grant said. "The Coast Guard will be here any minute. In the meantime, the worst boat is always better than the best life raft." He hoped that the mariners' maxim never to abandon ship too early would satisfy the group. He didn't want to tell them that the promenade was too high above the water to safely jump into a raft, or that shimmying down the side on fire hoses would be a feat too difficult for many of them to accomplish. The fact was that the only safe embarkation doors to the rafts were located on the freight deck, and with shooters on the 'tween decks and a possible truck bomb on the stern, the freight deck was definitely not a safe place for the passengers.

Grant went down to the freight deck on the starboard midship stairs, opposite the 'tween deck from where the shooters were located. He found the watertight door to the engine blocked from the inside, but one of the escape scuttles was wide open. He descended into the shadows and eerie silence and found Bo in the glow of the emergency lighting at the watertight door to the generator room.

"Bo," he said. "Are you okay?"

"I guess I'm okay," Bo said. "But there's a feller down here who ain't doing so good—he's caught between Satan and my better angel."

"What?" Grant said. Then he saw the big man caught in the partially closed door. It had squeezed his torso to half the size it was before. There was little blood, but this was obviously a mortal injury, with severe internal consequences. Only the pressure of the door itself was keeping the big man from bleeding to death, like a colossal mechanical tourniquet.

"Get me out of here," Behr said, as if he was not hurt at all. "Let me go."

"You see," Bo said, "the devil is telling me to twist this knob and cut this sinner in half. But my better angel is saying 'no, it's wrong to kill a man.'"

"Bo, forget him," Grant said. "We need your help on the freight deck."

"No, I can't," Bo said. "Holding a man's fate in your hand is a fearsome thing, Grant. Do I open the door or close it?

"Bo, he's damn near cut in half," Grant said. "If you open the door, he'll bleed to death in seconds anyway. Leave him here to think about dying."

"Fuck you!" Behr said. "You're dead, too. You're all dead."

"How do you figure that?" Grant said. "Your pals are dead or trapped. They are making their last stand right now. No matter what, we are not going to let them get to the catering truck. It's all over for you."

"Ha!" Behr said. "You idiots! That truck is going to blow this boat to hell. I packed it full of mixed fertilizer and diesel fuel myself, on top of two dozen propane bottles. Serves you right for screwing up the perfect plan. We had those wealthy pricks in the yacht club dead nuts in our sights until you idiots screwed this whole thing up. You morons! We almost brought the New World Order to their knees. Don't you get it? They are not talking about computers—they're plotting the final stages of their One World Government right now. You screwed up our plan, but you're going to get what you deserve—the timer is set and no power on Earth can stop it now!"

"You don't have time for crazy talk," Bo said. "You best be saying the Lord's Prayer about now."

"Oh no," Grant said, looking at Bo. "That is crazy talk. But this animal just might be telling the truth about the truck." He turned to Behr. "What time is that thing going to explode?"

"You'd like to know, wouldn't you?" Behr said. "You can't stop it now, so what the hell do I care? That truck will blow at ten o'clock, on the dot."

"That's only twenty minutes after we were due to arrive on Nantucket," Grant said.

"No shit," Behr said. "We figured we could get off the boat and park that truck behind the yacht club in twenty minutes. But you had to go and screw the whole thing up. But that is okay, because do you know what I did? I knew we would never get to Nantucket in time. Before I came down here, I cut the air lines to the brakes on that truck, just so nobody could move it. It is staying on this boat, no matter what. And you are going to get blown to hell. How smart are you now?"

"Oh my God," Grant said to Bo. "He might be telling the truth."

"While we're breathing, we've still got hope," Bo said. He turned to Behr and said, "You can stay right there. You better make your peace with God. You only need a few seconds to accept Jesus as your savior. Otherwise, I do not want to be here to meet Satan when he comes for you. Amen."

15

BLAZE OF GLORY

The 'Tween Deck

Katarina sat on the gritty nonskid paint behind the last car parked on the portside 'tween deck. Behind her, the boat's large open stern framed a scene of cold fog and diffuse light over gray water, while the remainder of the freight deck toward the bow was cloaked in shadows. The catering truck that Zack had driven onto the boat was below her on the freight deck, thirty feet away. Her heart swelled each time she heard Damien's voice, even though his reasoned words did little to quell Matthias's animal rage, and she held firm to the belief that he would still be her savior.

Until then, Katarina knew, she would have to help herself.

Her captors crouched on either side, aiming their weapons around the car and into the lines of parked autos and shadows deeper into the *Nighthawk*'s cavernous belly. Matthias held the girl in the plaid skirt so forcefully that his fist raised welts on her fair skin. "Shut up!" he said, stupidly believing that his brutish words could control her shaking and sobbing, which would not subside.

Katarina reached for the girl when Matthias pushed her away, and she took her in her arms. "It's going to be okay," she said. She pushed the girl's head down to her bosom, clear of the shotgun at her own neck. "Hold on to me. What is your name?" Katarina said.

The girl's shaking was palpable, as if she were being continuously shocked by high-voltage current. She might be old enough to be in high school, Katarina guessed, with curly auburn hair and bright blue eyes. Between sobbing, she said "Penny," over and over again.

"Penny?" Katarina said. "What a pretty name."

"No," the girl said, through sobbing. "Penny is my dog. I want Penny."

"Oh, but what is your name?"

"Gail. My name is Gail."

"Okay, Gail. I'm Katarina." She looked at Colt. His left hand was still firmly taped to the trigger of the shotgun at her neck, while he peered intently into the shadows, holding his Kalashnikov's pistol grip with his free hand. She noticed that his free arm seemed to be tiring from holding the assault rifle with only one hand. The boy was averting his eyes away from her, breathing heavily. She synchronized her breathing with his. He was trying to keep his focus on their pursuers, who were taking cover five cars away, with little success. He repeatedly looked over Katarina's head to Matthias, barely noticing Gail, desperately seeking approval and reassurance from the leader.

He was a good-looking kid. She guessed that he was even well-mannered under normal circumstances. It was the shotgun between them that was ugly, even more odious than the weapons that the attackers held in their hands. *It is so odd*, she thought—her father had kept a similar shotgun on top of a cupboard in their kitchen—loaded and ready in the event of a wolf attacking their animals. He used it to put food on their table. It was nothing more than one of the tools hanging in the shed, and it was used more often than most. Yet this sweet boy held this nearly identical thing as an object of unimaginable evil, pressed at her neck like the Devil's pitchfork.

"Cover me," Matthias said. The leader tensed, ready to make a move. He looked at Colt when he said. "Are you okay, boy?"

Colt nodded, full of bravado, and said, "Hell yes."

"I'm going to advance on the enemy," Matthias said. "If I get a shot off at them, you come out shooting. Got it?" Colt nodded again and Matthias crept around the car. Colt looked toward where their pursuers were hiding. Then Matthias was also out of sight.

Nothing happened.

Colt was breathing even harder. Katarina paced her breaths with his and made each of her inhalations and exhalations louder. He turned and looked at her. She felt his hand trembling on the shotgun when their eyes met. The boy was terrified. He noticed Gail and their eyes met—perhaps for the first time—but she quickly turned away in fear and revulsion.

Katarina touched his knee with her fingertips. Slowly, carefully, she pressed her right palm against him. Tears were welling in his pale gray eyes. The shotgun's safety was still on. They breathed together. She reached up and placed her left hand on his, around the shotgun's trigger. Their eyes remained locked while she picked at the end of the tape. She peeled the sticky strip away slowly, unwinding it from the trigger and his hand. His tears came when the tape was finally removed and she pressed one hand over his on the shotgun—*keep this hand here, so Matthias will not notice that I am free*—while she wiped his cheek with the other hand.

Matthias was agitated when he rushed back to them, staying low. "Damnit! They almost got me," he said. He spoke excitedly, quickly chopping the words. "You're keeping me alive, boy. You hear? They had a shot and they didn't take it. Had me dead nuts. I was looking right down the barrel of a damn gun. They knew you would blow her goddamn head off. That's why they let me get away."

What Matthias saw next changed everything.

The Coast Guard Cutter *Hammerhead* materialized out of the fog to make a slow pass at the *Nighthawk*'s stern, like a killer shark casting a wary sideways glance at his prey before turning back to strike. The sleek white patrol boat with a racing stripe at the bow was barely moving as it cruised in from the starboard side and disappeared into the fog to the port side, but not before Matthias and Colt saw a heavily armed boarding party standing ready. Colt's jaw dropped when he saw the two .50 caliber machine guns mounted on the cutter's bow. The heavy weapons were manned by helmeted crewmen—and one of the guns was aimed directly at him and Matthias.

The Hammerhead

"Mike, you're going to be on your own," Jack said to his chief engineer, five minutes before the *Hammerhead* arrived on scene, while the ferry was still miles away and hidden in the fog. "After I put your team on the *Nighthawk*, I might have to leave you to find the passengers who jumped overboard. We'll launch Neal in the small boat to help round them up. I've been talking to the ferry's mate on the radio, and he says there might be people as far as a mile away. They don't have long in this cold water."

"Go do your thing, Jack," Mike said. "The boarding team knows what we have to do." Mike rubbed the stubble on his chin. He usually shaved at night, when he showered to wash away the sweat and grime of the engine room, so his jaw was often sandpaper rough during a workday. "The only thing that bothers me is the hostages. This might get really messy."

"Sorry, Mike," Jack said. "I know I'm serving up a shit sandwich. You're going to have to just choke it down, buddy."

"This whole thing is a shit show," Mike said. "Is that mate on the *Nighthawk* sure these are homegrown terrorists?"

"He's absolutely positive," Jack said. "They had Michigan license plates on their truck, dressed like regular working stiffs. He said that only two of them are left—a bearded white guy with body armor and a bad habit of murdering people, and a fresh-faced kid with an AK-47."

"I've got to tell you, Jack," Mike said. "That really frosts my nuts." Mike had done two tours with the flotilla of US Coast Guard patrol boats operating in the Persian Gulf, boarding small vessels smuggling weapons and playing chicken with Iranian gunboats making threating moves. "Nothing pisses me off like white-trash assholes shooting up my own backyard while I was over there going toe-to-toe with those Al-Qaeda douchebags."

"I hear you," Jack said. He pointed to the radar. "There they are, about a thousand yards off the bow. I'm going to slow down and crawl past the stern before I put you onboard on the port side. We might even get a look at the shooters." He turned to the quartermaster and said, "Put up the battle flag. It helps me get in the mood for this shit."

"I like it," Mike said after the quartermaster went out of the pilothouse to run up an over-size American flag on the *Hammerhead's* mast. "Get really close, Jack. Let us let these jerkwads know we're loaded for bear."

They were only three hundred yards away when they sighted the *Nighthawk* visually. The big ferry was dead in the water with a few large circular life rafts alongside, tethered to the ship. There were only a handful of people in the rafts, although more than a hundred people in red life jackets were on the bow. Some of them stood up and cheered when they sighted the patrol boat with the racing stripe and the American flag coming out of the fog.

Mike looked through the binoculars as they went past the stern. He could see the attackers and their hostages behind the last car on the 'tween deck. Matthias might have taken a shot at the *Hammerhead* as it passed the stern—except that the sight of the .50 caliber Browning machine gun that was manned and ready on the bow convinced him to reconsider.

"Yeah, that's right," Mike said, when he got a good look at Matthias's face through the binoculars. "I'm coming for you, asshole."

"A crewman is going to meet you at the mid-ship boarding door," Jack said as he turned the *Hammerhead* to the *Nighthawk's* port side. "Just one more thing, look what's headed our way—fast." He pointed to the radar, where a broken mass of blue, red, and gold was inching across the screen. "That squall line is going to be on us real soon. It's getting pushed by forty-five-knot winds, so get ready for some wild weather."

"Right," Mike said. "What else could go wrong?" He cinched the strap on his red boarding helmet and tested the team radio circuit as he went down to the deck where his five men were standing by. "Everybody hear me okay?" he said. He got five thumbs-up and reviewed his team. He had four solid guys going with him. Carter was a shrimper from the Outer Banks who handled the shotgun like he was born with a 12 gauge in his crib. Nelson and Blackie were squared-away sailors with M-16s, and Vernon was generally an annoying hyperactive black kid from inner-city Detroit, but Mike was glad to have his street smarts on the team. The new kid was number five, and he would not have been his first choice, but he was qualified with the M-16—on paper, anyway.

Mike said, "Barnes, how many times have you boarded a suspect vessel?"

"This is the first time, Chief."

"Great," Mike said, even though it was not. "Stay close to Nelson and Blackie. Keep your eyes and ears open and be ready for anything." Mike looked in Barnes's eyes and gave a wry grin as he tugged on the M-16 in his hands. "And for Christ sakes, don't shoot me in the back with this thing."

The *Nighthawk*'s mid-ship boarding door was open when Jack brought the *Hammerhead* alongside. The door was only six feet above the waterline, just above the ferry's rub-rail, at the perfect height for the team to step across. A crewman in a blue shirt was standing by.

You never know, Mike thought, as he got ready to step onto the *Nighthawk*. He'd boarded hundreds of boats—fishermen just trying to make a living, and open scows overloaded with hundreds of Haitians trying new lives for Florida, and long-liners with hidden compartments crammed with marijuana, and Arab dhows with concealed howitzer rounds to be converted into roadside bombs—and all he knew was that you never know.

Carter held the shotgun at high-port and pumped a round into the chamber before he and Mike stepped across the rail, which was not kosher according to the standard operating procedures. Then again, nothing about this boarding was standard, Mike thought as he stepped into the deep shadows of the *Nighthawk*'s freight deck, just as two shots from a high-power rifle echoed off the steel bulkheads and around the parked cars and trucks.

The 'Tween Deck

When the *Hammerhead* crossed the *Nighthawk*'s stern, Katarina knew she was running out of time. The authorities had arrived and there was no reason to doubt that they were already coming aboard the *Nighthawk*, armed to the hilt. When Matthias said, "Blaze of glory," she realized that he intended to end his rampage in a firestorm of violence that would consume her and this innocent young girl, Gail—unless she managed to escape in the next few moments.

"Matthias, it's all over," she heard Damien say from the shadows three cars ahead. "Those Coast Guard boys are trigger-happy. This is your last chance. My family owns the ferry company, Matthias. We have many lawyers, good lawyers. Let the women go, and we will use every one of those lawyers to make sure you get a fair trial. The whole world will be watching and listening to your every word. Isn't that what you want? How about it?"

"Think about it," Katarina said to Matthias. "Damien is a man of his word, and his family is very powerful."

"Shut up, bitch!" Matthias said. He turned toward Damien and said, "Screw off!" Then he held his AK-47 over his head and fired two rounds blindly with his thumb on the trigger, shattering what little glass remained in the cars between the warring parties. He turned to Colt next, and he said, "Blaze of glory, boy. Blaze of glory! But we can't stay here. We're totally exposed if those storm troopers on that government boat make another pass at us." He pointed at a small alcove in an aft corner of the freight deck. "Remember that place, Colt? We saw it on one of our recon missions on this boat. Remember? They keep big ropes and stuff in there. That is the final bunker. That is where we make our stand for liberty. You follow me and bring those bitches!"

Matthias leapt off the 'tween deck onto the roof of a Mercedes-Benz parked below, setting off the automobile's alarm siren. "Come on, boy! Blaze of glory!"

Colt turned to Katarina when she tugged his wrist away from the shotgun's trigger. "Don't go," she said, when the shotgun was out of Colt's hands, hanging like a satanic pendant in front of her. "Stay with me." Gail turned to look at Colt then, and she recoiled in terror and revulsion at the sight of him, which profoundly affected the boy. His eyes teared, and he turned to follow his messiah. "No! You're not bad," Katarina said, holding the boy back by his sleeve. "You're not evil like Matthias. I know you're not."

The sleeve of his shirt ripped in her grasp as he pulled away, the fabric rending as the stitches at the seam broke free, exposing a swastika and "14 Words" tattooed on his forearm.

"Oh my God," Katarina said. "What have they done to you?"

Colt did not look back before he followed Matthias down to the freight deck. The leader dove into the steel alcove first, from which they would have a secure bunker to cover all approaches to the catering truck. The boy, however, paused at the doorway to their final lair with his assault rifle in his hands and turned to look up at Katarina and Gail on the 'tween deck. Just as Damien and Lou came around the cars and arrived at their sides.

The boy froze when Lou raised his assault rifle on the 'tween deck and took a bead on the center of his teenage chest. He knew that the 7.62mm steel-jacketed ammunition would easily cleave though the light Kevlar vest he wore and pierce his heart—except that Katarina reached up to swat the Kalashnikov aside as Lou fired.

The round went wild, and Colt ducked into the alcove with Matthias, unscathed.

Lou cursed at Katarina for interfering with his shot, then he too jumped down to the freight deck. He stayed low behind the trucks in the center lane and moved into a position where he could fire into the rope locker.

Then Damien was pulling the kill-noose off Katarina's neck. She felt his warmth when he wrapped his arms around her and they embraced in a writhing, tearful, sloppy kiss that released a torrent of agony from her soul.

The Freight Deck

The two shots from Matthias's AK-47 were still echoing on the freight deck when Dylan met the Coast Guard boarding team at the midship embarkation door. "What took you so long?" he said.

Chief Mike ignored the question. "How many shooters are there?" he said. "Where are the bad guys and where are your guys?"

"I'm not sure," Dylan said. "Our crew has two of the assholes pinned down on the port 'tween deck, back by the stern. They have our delicatessen supervisor as a hostage. That's all I know."

Mike turned to his team. "Sounds like those guys we saw on the 'tween deck as we went by the stern. Nelson and Blackie, take Barnes and work your way aft on the freight deck. Stay in cover as much as possible, and do not shoot the damn hostages. Carter and Vernon, you are with me on the 'tween deck."

The boarding team heard Lou's shot that missed Colt as they moved aft. They had not gone far when they met Katarina and Gail rushing toward them. "Thank God you're here," Katarina said. "Don't shoot the boy, Colt. He helped us escape."

Mike said, "Were you the woman they were holding as a hostage?"

"Yes," Katarina said. "The crew just helped us get free."

"Where are the bad guys now?" Mike said.

"Matthias jumped down to the freight deck and went into the rope storage locker at the stern. So did Colt."

Mike relayed this information to the team on their helmet radios. He kept moving aft and found Damien and Sean at the aft end of the 'tween deck, with their weapons trained on the opening to the storage area. "You can put those weapons down," Mike said. "We'll take it from here."

"I don't think we can disarm ourselves yet," Damien said. "We've been fighting for our lives, and you're coming late to the party."

"Hey, Chief," Sean said. "I'm a cop, and I'm not dropping my weapon for anybody. The bad guys are all in the stern rope locker. Tell your guys not to shoot the ferry crewman with an AK-47 down on the freight deck."

"What's he doing down there?" Mike said after he relayed the information to Nelson, Blackie, and Barnes on the freight deck.

"He's outflanking these assholes," Sean said. "He's making your job a lot easier if you don't shoot him by accident."

"Okay, everybody, relax," Mike said. "We'll evacuate the boat and wait these guys out. They can't stay in that little space for too long."

By then Grant and Bo had come up from the engine room. Bo met Lou on the freight deck and they both took cover behind the flatbed tractor trailer that was ahead of the catering truck, while Grant came up to the 'tween deck. "We have a big problem," he said when he reached Damien and the others. "That truck is rigged to explode in about ten minutes."

"Who are you?" Mike said

"Grant Butler. I'm the mate."

"No, he's the captain now," Damien said. "I'm Damien Dalzell, one of the owners and managers of the company." He turned back to Grant and said, "Did you find the big man in the engine room?"

"Yes," Grant said. "Bo cut him down to size."

"Okay," Mike said. "What's this about a bomb?"

"That's what we heard from the guy they called Behr, down in the engine room," Grant said. "He's probably dead by now, but he was the one who told us that truck was rigged to explode at ten o'clock."

"Shit," Sean said. He looked at his father's old watch on his wrist. "That's only twelve minutes. We do not have time to screw around. Some of the wounded are directly above us and can't be moved."

"Damnit," Mike said. "Our helicopters are having a hard time getting through the fog and thunderstorms. Hoisting injured people is a tricky operation and it takes a lot of time. And I know the Airedales won't like the idea of hovering above shooters and a bomb."

"That's not enough time to evacuate the boat anyway," Damien said. "I don't suppose the Coast Guard knows how to diffuse a truck bomb?"

"I haven't got a clue," Mike said.

"Right," Damien said, looking at Grant. "We're running out of time. Are you thinking what I'm thinking, Captain?"

"I am," Grant said. "But I wish I wasn't." He had spent years taking all the precautions to secure vehicles so they couldn't fall off the stern of the boat. So what he said next was against all his instincts. "We've got to get that catering truck off the boat."

"Huh? What are you talking about?" Mike said. "You want to jettison that truck?"

"Now you're talking," Sean said. "Let's push that sucker off the stern."

"There's one more thing I have to tell you," Grant said. "The big man in the engine room told us that he cut the air lines to the brakes. We'll have to release the air brakes the hard way if we want to move that truck."

"We can do that," Damien said. "If we have time."

Sean said, "Let's stop screwing around and do this."

"Okay," Mike said. "That is a crazy idea, but I'm with you. First, we have to neutralize those two in the locker. Let's go get them."

The Hammerhead

After Jack put the boarding team on the *Nighthawk*, he launched Neal in the rescue boat to search for survivors in the water while he loitered near the ferry, close enough to listen in on the boarding team's helmet radios. When he heard the boarding team talking about a possible truck bomb and two shooters taking positions in a rope locker, he steered the *Hammerhead* around to the ferry's stern to see for himself.

The squall line was passing through by then, darkening the sky with sporadic bursts of hard rain and furious winds that whipped wavelets into steep, closely spaced whitecaps. Jack hove-to thirty yards off the *Nighthawk*'s stern and put his own transom into the maelstrom, using an occasional shot astern on one of his engines to reverse-weathervane and hold position, which was a lot easier than struggling to hold the bow into the wind—and it kept the .50 caliber machine guns on his bow pointed at the attackers.

Framed in the broad open stern under the sundeck, the freight deck looked like a stage where a desperate scene was unfolding. Jack saw his crewmen approaching behind parked cars and trucks. When Mike gave the word on their radios, they commenced firing, turning the interior of the alcove into a hornet's nest of rounds ricocheting off the steel bulkheads. It did not seem like anyone inside the locker could possibly survive this fusillade, but the attackers kept firing back at the boarding team.

Jack looked at the alcove through his binoculars and knew that this assault was futile, because the attackers had taken refuge inside the coils of heavy hawsers in the alcove. The ropes around them were absorbing the bullets while they raised their weapons over their heads to blindly fire at Mike's boarding team.

Jack raised the microphone of his radio and pushed the transmit button. "Call it off, Mike," he said. "That's not going to work."

"Damnit!" Jack said, when he saw one of his men go down on the freight deck. The binoculars put him close to the action, and it looked like Nelson had been hit in the thigh. There was a lot of blood.

"Good man, Barnes!" Jack said, when he saw another crewman pulling Nelson out of the field of fire.

The wound above Nelson's knee looked bad. He could bleed to death, Jack knew, if he did not get to a trauma center soon. His wife was six months pregnant back in the base housing area, and the thought flashed though Jack's mind that someone was going to have to knock on her door and tell her what had happened to her husband on what should have been a routine patrol.

Now, it was personal.

"Mike, get everyone clear," he said into the radio. "Move everybody far forward, way up there. I'm going to end this thing!"

He jammed the throttles down and the *Hammerhead* jumped ahead with a roar from the diesels. "Spokes, get on the helm," he said to the quartermaster. "Take me around the port side and turn toward the *Nighthawk*'s stern. Put our bow toward their stern at a thirty-degree angle, dead slow speed. Got it?"

The quartermaster understood perfectly what was about to happen when Jack bolted out of the pilothouse and sprang down to the main deck with his dress hat still on. He pushed the two crewmen manning the portside .50 caliber machine gun aside and took the two grips in his hands. Spokes brought the *Hammerhead* around beautifully as Jack pulled the big handle back to slam a round into the chamber and sighted the barrel onto the steel plating on the *Nighthawk*'s stern. They were only fifteen yards away when he pressed the butterfly trigger between the grips with his thumbs. The fearsome weapon barked twice and spit heavy brass casings onto the deck. Two large punctures appeared in the crisp white paint on the ferry, two feet above the height of the freight deck. Jack squeezed the trigger again and the killing machine barked three times, then four times, then three times again, and again. The linked ammunition jumped out of the can on the left side of the gun and flew out of the right side as a blur of empty casings. Again, and again.

When he ceased firing and raised the cover on the receiver to clear the action, the steel plating outside the storage alcove was buckled and riddled with large holes. Jack raised a fist at the utter destruction he had caused, and he said, "Don't fuck with my boys!"

16

THE BITTER END

The Freight Deck

Delquan Vernon had grown up on the south side of Chicago, and he would probably still be there if he had not been bussed to a youth sailing program on Lake Michigan one Saturday afternoon when he was fourteen years old. That day when he first went onto Lake Michigan in a sailing dinghy was the first moment in his young life when his horizon was not limited by the hard facades of an urban landscape. He spent much of his free time after that in the sailing program, working on the boats and becoming an instructor, and eventually enlisting in the US Coast Guard.

Vernon had seen a lot on the city streets and in the projects, but he had never seen anything like what he saw when he peered into the rope storage alcove on the stern of the *Nighthawk*. The carnage of the chopped-up bodies before him—severed arms and legs and intestines spilling from ruptured torsos and half a head, neatly split like a coconut—was astounding and unsettling. The shrapnel from the holes blown into the boat's exterior hull plating by the *Hammerhead*'s .50 caliber machine gun had turned the interior of the alcove into a meat grinder.

"Vernon!" Chief Mike said. "Quit gawking and get over here."

The boat's crew and the boarding team were working to get the catering truck off the stern. Lou had cast his AK-47 aside. He was taking down the chains and stanchions that crossed the freight deck at the stern to keep people from falling overboard when the boat was under way. The windblown wavelets on the surface of the saltwater rose up to the freight deck and lapped at his feet. Hard rain was pouring in.

Sean was in his own van, breaking the ignition lock on the steering column with a screwdriver while cursing that Helen still had the key. When he could force the transmission into neutral, he jumped out of the vehicle. Vernon helped him and Lou push the van off the stern, where it floated against the boat's transom for what seemed like a long time before it sank into the waves.

"What's the holdup?" Lou said, when they stood alongside the catering truck.

"They cut the lines to the air brakes," Damien said. "We're going to have to release them the hard way."

"No problem," Bo said, brandishing a set of vise-grips. "All we have to do is cage the brakes."

"How do we do that?"

"One of you grab another wrench for the other side," Bo said, as he crawled under the truck's rear axle. "I'll show you."

"We're running out of time," Grant said as he joined Bo under the axle. "If this doesn't work—"

"It will work," Bo said. "See these cans behind the axle?" There were two on each side, one for each of the double rear wheels. "Take the nut off the bolt mounted to the side of the can. Then we take the bolt and insert it into the back of the can. There are two locking lugs that hold it in. See how easy that is? Do not forget the washer, because we're going to tighten down on this nut and pull the piston back inside the can. Then the brakes are released, so be careful—the truck will be free to roll after that."

"I hate to tell you this," Sean said. "This truck isn't rolling anywhere. It has flat tires after all the bullets that those assholes were firing toward us."

"Damn, I didn't notice that," Grant said as he finished caging the brakes and got out from under the truck. "We'll have to try. We might be able to muscle it off if we all put our backs into it."

"You're cutting it really close," Lou said. "What time did you say this thing was going to blow?"

"We've only got a minute or two," Grant said. He put his back against the front bumper and pushed with his legs. "Let's try it."

Damien and Lou joined Grant with their backs against the truck's front bumper, followed by Mike's boarding team. Even Bo added his lean frame to the effort, but with all of them pushing, the truck would not budge on the flat tires.

Grant looked to the crewmen at his side and shook his head. *It is too damn late,* he thought. *I have totally screwed this up. My shipmates and a whole lot of other people are going to die when this truck explodes because I made the wrong decisions.* He was about to tell them all to give up and run for their lives when he heard the roar of twin diesel engines winding up, close to where they were struggling.

Jack had brought the *Hammerhead* around to the stern of the *Nighthawk,* and he saw what had to be done. He split the throttles—one hard ahead and the other hard reverse—to spin the transom of the patrol boat around, stopping one or two feet from the ferry, stern to stern. He had sent Spokes down to pass a towline to the crew on the ferry. The gusty wind was tossing the patrol boat around and waves jumped up in the narrow gap between the two vessels, creating a scene akin to ice floes jostling in a raging river.

"Vernon, take this," Spokes said, when he tossed the braided nylon hawser to the freight deck. "Wrap it around the axle on that truck!"

The *Hammerhead*'s propeller wash joined with the choppy seas to splash water around Vernon's feet when he grabbed the bitter end of the towline. Lou dove under the truck with him and they wrapped four round turns of the hawser around the axle and secured the thimble and shackle on the bitter end to the truck's chassis.

"Go!" Lou waved when he and Vernon jumped up.

Jack idled away from the *Nighthawk* and paid out two hundred feet of towline before he told Spokes to make the hawser fast to the towing bitt. He feathered the throttles in and out of gear to take a steady strain on the towline, working the power up until the *Hammerhead*'s diesels were screaming. The catering truck budged and hesitated for scant seconds before it rolled unevenly off the freight deck at the stern.

Jack kept the patrol boat's engines powered up after the truck splashed off the back of the ferry. It followed the *Hammerhead* half-submerged, like a drunken water skier who wouldn't let go, rolling and spinning and in a jerking, spastic slide, until Jack eased the throttles back and ordered Spokes to bring an axe down on the hawser.

"Thank you, God," Bo said, when the *Hammerhead* and the sinking truck were two hundred yards away from where they stood on the freight deck.

"That was too close," Lou said. "What time is it?"

Sean looked at his wristwatch. "I have ten o'clock," he said. "How about you, Grant?"

"Yup, ten on the dot," Grant said, reading the time off his cell phone. "It should blow any second."

EPILOGUE

The Freight Deck

Jeez, it didn't blow," Lou said, a few minutes after the *Hammerhead* released the towline, allowing the truck to float away and disappear into the water of Nantucket Sound. "The damn truck didn't blow."

"Maybe the detonator failed," Grant said. "Or maybe the water got to it."

Damien said, "Maybe there never was a bomb."

"Maybe it was all bullshit," Sean said. "Anyway, see you guys later. I've got to go find Helen and tell her I pushed her van off the boat—for a bomb that didn't go off." He walked away laughing. "She really loved that van."

The thunder-squalls had cleared the fog as they pushed through, leaving calm seas and sunshine in its wake. "Honest to God," Lou said. "If I see a rainbow, I'm going to puke."

"There's your rainbow," Bo said as a large Coast Guard helicopter moved into a hovering position over the sundeck and began hoisting the injured passengers. Highland Steamboat's other big boat, the *Shearwater*, was approaching rapidly and Grant spoke into his portable radio to arrange for them to come alongside to evacuate the passengers.

When Dylan, Butch, and Justin joined them, all the *Nighthawk*'s surviving crew—except for Dana—were mustered on the stern.

185

"I can't believe it," Butch said. "Is it really over?"

"Yup," Dylan said. "It seemed to last for hours. But it all happened so fast."

"It's over," Grant said. He absentmindedly reached for a cigarette but only found an empty shirt pocket. "And it all happened in less than forty minutes. I keep thinking the clock in my cell phone stopped, but it's true—about thirty-six minutes ago we turned around, and all this started."

"It seems like an eternity," Justin said.

"Is Tommy really gone?" Butch said. "Is anybody sure?"

"He's gone," Justin said. "Sweet Jesus, he's gone."

"And Saint and Tony, too," Dylan said. "I saw both up there. Damn it, I wish I had not, but I saw them both."

Katarina came to the stern and stood alongside Damien. They stood in the clear air after the storm front had passed and felt the sunshine on their faces. He put his arm around her, and it felt good to stand in the open with the woman he loved. He said, "How is that girl in the plaid skirt?"

"Gail will be okay," Katarina said. "Except for the loss of her dog."

"Katarina, you were with them the whole time," Grant said. "What did they want from us?"

"Revenge," Katarina said. "All I heard from Matthias was hate."

"Revenge for what?" Butch said. "We didn't do anything to him."

"You didn't share his vision of the world," Bo said. "Put a gun in some men's hands, and you're either with them or against them. It's as simple as that."

"I think they were just stupid," Dylan said. "They were just idiots with guns and nothing to lose. All that New World Order conspiracy nonsense is just stupid."

"I don't know," Justin said. "There are lots of folks who aren't happy about the way things are going in this country. People don't like all the changes. Maybe these assholes almost started something big."

"No way," Lou said. "There isn't going to be any race war, or class war, or whatever you want to call it. This country almost stumbled in the Sixties, but we pulled back from the brink. We always pull back, after people come to their senses and calm down."

"I wish I could be so sure about that," Bo said. "There's a lot of anger right now. We're like two countries, at war with ourselves."

The *Nighthawk*'s decks were crawling with law enforcement personnel and rescue workers by then. They had arrived by helicopter and by State Police boats and Coast Guard cutters, and the ferry *Shearwater* was alongside, taking the passengers off.

Chief Mike came back to the stern. He looked at Grant and said, "How is your passenger count coming?"

"We can't account for fourteen people," Grant said.

"The company will put everyone up in a hotel," Damien said. "We'll have to get all the information, for our insurance company. Everyone is going to have to give statements, of course."

"You'd better believe it," Mike said. "This whole boat is a major crime scene. The FBI is going to have a field day putting this puzzle together, but they'll figure out exactly what happened." Mike scratched his chin. "Then again, the whole asshole casserole of high-ranking officials is going to show up with creased trousers and Gucci shoes to do the press conference for the TV cameras. That's okay." He laughed, before he walked away. "As long as George Clooney plays my part in the movie."

"I hadn't even thought of that," Lou said. "I guess this is going to be a big news story."

"Right," Grant said. "We're going to look pretty stupid for pushing a truck that didn't explode off the stern."

"The Monday morning quarterbacks will come at us hard," Dylan said. "They always do."

"They just better not say one damn bad word about Tommy," Justin said. "I swear, not one bad word about Tommy."

"Or Saint," Lou said. "Or Tony. I don't care what they say about me, but I won't stand for one bad word about our guys."

"That boy Todd?" Bo said. "That little Sea Sprout. I do not much care what anybody says, that was a fine young man. Nothing can change that."

"Don't worry about it," Damien said. "My father is an ace at shooting down news reporters. You guys did a great job. Nobody could have done more."

"I wish I could believe that," Grant said. "People are going to ask how seven terrorists could buy tickets and maybe drive a truck bomb onto the boat. I guess that's going to be on me."

"What about Judd?" Lou said. "That dope didn't do his job."

"The government dropped the ball," Dylan said. "A little warning would have changed everything."

"The company would have shut all the boats down if there was a hint of trouble," Damien said. "It wouldn't be worth running if creditable threats had been detected."

"I'm still the sap who took their tickets and let them on the boat," Grant said.

"You weren't looking for a militia of neo-Nazis," Damien said. "We're all spring-loaded to detect groups of Middle Eastern terrorists before they strike, but all the domestic terror attackers have been lone wolf killers. Even the Oklahoma City bombing was carried out by one idiot. This is something new—a mass attack by our own citizens. We're going to have to defend ourselves against armies of homegrown storm troopers from now on."

"It's not new to me," Bo said. "Only thing is—now the KKK boys are attacking white folks."

"Look at this," Butch said, pointing out over the water. "Look at who is coming."

Dana chugged alongside the *Nighthawk*'s stern in the rescue boat, towing a life raft with survivors. The kid in the Roger Williams sweatshirt was seated in the bow of the small boat, as far forward as a person could go.

"How many?" Grant said.

"I count fourteen," Dana said. "That's all I could find."

"Fourteen is perfect," Grant said. "Strong work, Dana. Take them straight to the *Shearwater* for the trip back to Hyannis."

The distant sound of the catering truck exploding underwater came suddenly, as a loud *Whoosh*-BOOM! "Whoa," Justin said, as the sound echoed through the freight deck and came back to them.

"Son of a gun," Lou said. "There was a bomb, after all."

"We were lucky," Grant said.

"No," Damien said. "You made all the right decisions. What this crew did was above and beyond. Now we've got to make sure it never happens again."

Dana was about to pull away with the rescue boat when the kid in the Roger Williams sweatshirt called to Grant. "Look what I found," he said. The head and front paws of a terrier with bright eyes and alert ears emerged from the collar of his sweatshirt like a chick from an egg. "This puppy almost landed on my head after I jumped. She rode on my shoulders until Dana came along. Can I keep her?"

"Nope," Grant said. "That dog's owner is still crying her eyes out. You'll find her with the rest of the passengers when you get aboard the *Shearwater*—and you'll make a girl in a plaid skirt incredibly happy."

"Sure, I'll find her," the kid said, with a smile and a shrug. "After all, who doesn't like a happy ending?"

AFTERWORD

The "breaking news" networks chanted about "The Miracle on Nantucket Sound" for days after the attack, breathlessly reporting that all two hundred and five passengers aboard the ferry *Nighthawk* had survived the nightmare.

Four crewmembers and one security guard perished in the rampage, while six passengers and one Coast Guard seaman received serious injuries. Two of the attackers survived and are in federal custody facing charges of murder and piracy. A grand jury convened by the United States Attorney in Boston has declined to deliver indictments against any of the *Nighthawk* crewmembers and passengers who inflicted bodily harm on the attackers while suppressing the rampage.

Citing exclusions for acts of terrorism, Highland Steamboat Company's insurance carrier has balked at satisfying claims arising from the attack and is arguing in court to limit their liability. While the legal wrangling continues, Highland Steamboat has created an interim compensation fund for all persons affected by the rampage.

Horace Judd's widow excluded herself from the interim compensation fund by filing a separate wrongful death lawsuit alleging negligence by the crew of the *Nighthawk* in the death of her spouse. Highland Steamboat has vowed never to settle under those terms and the case is expected to languish in the courts for many years.

Jack Bramble retired from the Coast Guard and is now the captain of a ninety-foot Hatteras sport fishing boat in Key Largo, Florida, where he is a colorful fixture at the Ocean Reef Club. Chief Mike Barlow was reassigned to an office cubicle in Coast Guard Headquarters for his last year of active duty, where he is kept far away from journalists while collating and filing monthly fuel consumption reports in the bottom drawer of his desk.

The Nantucket harbormaster brought divers to rescue the trapped crewmen from an air pocket in the trawler *Nova Sintra*, which was later re-floated and repaired. Captain Geno Branca and Jorge Costa returned to the fishing grounds and continue to provide fresh seafood to markets and restaurants all over New England.

Sean Lamont is now a lieutenant in the NYPD assigned to uniform patrol in the Borough of Brooklyn. He and Helen attended Abbey and Ezra's wedding, while the twins and Olivia enjoy poring over road atlases to chart the route of a cross-country trip in the new luxury minivan that the Highland Steamboat Company purchased for their family.

Midshipman Todd Bell has been formally enshrined at the Merchant Mariners' Memorial overlooking the Cape Cod Canal in Buzzards Bay, Massachusetts. His portrait now hangs alongside those of Tom Chapman, Saint, and Tony, in the Highland Steamboat Company's main office.

Lou has returned to commercial fishing aboard a small lobster boat out of Stage Harbor in Chatham, Massachusetts. He rises early and sleeps well.

Grant and his wife are sailing in the Caribbean on their new boat. They have decided to transit through the Panama Canal into the Pacific Ocean next year. He recently sent a postcard to Bo asking him to go to the mate's stateroom on the *Nighthawk* and throw that last pack of cigarettes overboard.

Damien and Katarina were married in Provincetown two months after the rampage. He is dividing his time between revitalizing the family business and organizing his own independent marine consulting company, which will commence operations next year. In the meantime, he is supervising the design and construction of Highland Steamboat Company's powerful new ferry, to be christened the *Thomas Chapman*.

Bo, Dana, Justin, Dylan, and Butch continue to report for duty at the Highland Steamboat Company. In the months after the rampage they helped to repair the damage to the *Nighthawk*, which has returned to daily service between Hyannis and Nantucket. If you happen to see them on the run, they will only say, "Welcome aboard," and go quietly about keeping the schedule.

AUTHOR'S NOTE

June 25, 2020

Because I worked on the water for forty years, in the US Coast Guard and then on oceangoing workboats and coastal ferries like the *Nighthawk*, I approached this story with trepidation. I certainly did not wish to encourage any person or persons to try something stupid, and the idea that a copycat would use this story as a road map for violence aboard any vessel is repulsive to me—and ill-advised for any bad actor. I can safely say that since the 9/11 attacks and other senseless events in public places, the actual precautions and countermeasures employed by passenger vessels are many, discreet, and intentionally not mentioned here.

My goal was to tell a rip-roaring sea story—an adventure—full of raw action. To that end, *Rampage* is essentially a tale of twenty-first century professional mariners thrust into a seventeenth-century pirate attack upon a vessel. To those readers who might complain that the graphic nature of the violence herein was excessive or unwarranted, I would say that there is nothing gratuitous about good people struggling to survive amid the evil intents of extremists. Some would say it is the story of our times.

The first draft of this story featured Middle Eastern terrorists attacking an annual conference of academics and tech entrepreneurs on Nantucket. However, from a fiction author's point of view, domestic extremists are much more complex and interesting characters, and the televised sight of armed men parading on some statehouse steps—

195

dressed for battle with public officials—made the possibility of home-grown terrorists acting out their bizarre online fantasies of revenge, revolution, and civil strife seem slightly less far-fetched. All of which makes it necessary for me to say, dear reader, it is only fiction. I am not in the business of sounding warnings or predicting future events. I simply tell stories.

My gun owner friends, who are many, may question how I could postulate the absence of armed law-abiding citizens aboard the *Nighthawk*. I recognize that there have been many cases where citizens and off-duty military and law enforcement personnel have abruptly halted the hostile actions of a lone shooter, and that is a good thing. However, I doubt that an impromptu assembly of "good guys" with handguns could prevail against organized and determined attackers with assault rifles and body armor, in the chaos of a confined space full of innocent people. Also, the armed citizen narrative would have introduced a plethora of characters to be added to the story of the *Nighthawk*'s crew, and that might have been a prohibitively complex story for me to write. As a compromise I inserted the character of Sean Lamont—the young New York City cop from my first novel, *East River Trust*—into this story.

Finally, I will ask my professional mariner friends to forgive any factual atrocities I may have committed while splicing the details of our profession, both technical and mundane, into a fictional narrative for the reader. If I only got one thing right, shipmates, I hope it is this—when you are part of a solid crew, working on the water is as good as it gets.

Fair winds,

Doug Cooper
Bristol, Rhode Island
USA

Made in the USA
Middletown, DE
02 December 2020

26147109R00119